PRAISE F  T0029535

"Jess Lourey is a talented, witty, and clever writer."
—Monica Ferris, author of the Needlecraft Mysteries

"Don't miss this one—it's a hoot!"
—William Kent Krueger, *New York Times* bestselling author

"With just the right amount of insouciance, tongue-in-cheek sexiness, and plain common sense, Jess Lourey offers up a funny, well-written, engaging story . . . Readers will thoroughly enjoy the well-paced ride."
—Carl Brookins, author of *The Case of the Greedy Lawyers*

PRAISE FOR *MAY DAY*

"Jess Lourey writes about a small-town assistant librarian, but this is no genteel traditional mystery. Mira James likes guys in a big way, likes booze, and isn't afraid of motorcycles. She flees a dead-end job and a dead-end boyfriend in Minneapolis and ends up in Battle Lake, a little town with plenty of dirty secrets. The first-person narrative in *May Day* is fresh, the characters quirky. Minnesota has many fine crime writers, and Jess Lourey has just entered their ranks!"
—Ellen Hart, award-winning author of the Jane Lawless and Sophie Greenway series

"This trade paperback packed a punch . . . I loved it from the get-go!"
—*Tulsa World*

"What a romp this is! I found myself laughing out loud."
—*Crimespree Magazine*

"Mira digs up a closetful of dirty secrets, including sex parties, cross-dressing, and blackmail, on her way to exposing the killer. Lourey's debut has a likable heroine and surfeit of sass."
—*Kirkus Reviews*

PRAISE FOR *THE TAKEN ONES*

Short-listed for the 2024 Edgar Award for Best Paperback Original

"Setting the standard for top-notch thrillers, *The Taken Ones* is smart, compelling, and filled with utterly real characters. Lourey brings her formidable storytelling talent to the game and, on top of that, wows us with a deft stylistic touch. This is a one-sitting read!"
—Jeffery Deaver, author of *The Bone Collector* and *The Watchmaker's Hand*

"*The Taken Ones* has Jess Lourey's trademark of suspense all the way. A damaged and brave heroine, an equally damaged evildoer, and missing girls from long ago all combine to keep the reader rushing through to the explosive ending."
—Charlaine Harris, *New York Times* bestselling author

"Along with an incredible cast of support characters, *The Taken Ones* will break your heart wide open and stay with you long after you've turned the final page. This is a 2023 must read."
—Danielle Girard, *USA Today* and Amazon #1 bestselling author of *Up Close*

PRAISE FOR *THE QUARRY GIRLS*

Winner of the 2023 Anthony Award for Best Paperback Original

Winner of the 2023 Minnesota Book Award for Genre Fiction

"Few authors can blend the genuine fear generated by a sordid tale of true crime with evocative, three-dimensional characters and mesmerizing prose like Jess Lourey. Her fictional stories feel rooted in a world we all know but also fear. *The Quarry Girls* is a story of secrets gone to seed, and Lourey gives readers her best novel yet—which is quite the accomplishment. Calling it: *The Quarry Girls* will be one of the best books of the year."

—Alex Segura, acclaimed author of *Secret Identity, Star Wars Poe Dameron: Free Fall*, and *Miami Midnight*

"Jess Lourey once more taps deep into her Midwest roots and childhood fears with *The Quarry Girls*, an absorbing, true crime–informed thriller narrated in the compelling voice of young drummer Heather Cash as she and her bandmates navigate the treacherous and confusing ground between girlhood and womanhood one simmering and deadly summer. Lourey conveys the edgy, hungry restlessness of teen girls with a touch of Megan Abbott while steadily intensifying the claustrophobic atmosphere of a small 1977 Minnesota town where darkness snakes below the surface."

—Loreth Anne White, *Washington Post* and Amazon Charts bestselling author of *The Patient's Secret*

"Inspired by a true story, it's a creepy page-turner that has me eager to read more of Ms. Lourey's works, especially if they're all as incisive as this thought-provoking novel."

—Criminal Element

"*Bloodline* by Jess Lourey is a psychological thriller that grabbed me from the beginning and didn't let go."

—*Mystery & Suspense Magazine*

"*Bloodline* blends page-turning storytelling with clever homages to such horror classics as *Rosemary's Baby*, *The Stepford Wives*, and *Harvest Home*."

—*Toronto Star*

"*Bloodline* is a terrific, creepy thriller, and Jess Lourey clearly knows how to get under your skin."

—Bookreporter

"[A] tightly coiled domestic thriller that slowly but persuasively builds the suspense."

—*South Florida Sun Sentinel*

"I should know better than to pick up a new Jess Lourey book thinking I'll just peek at the first few pages and then get back to the book I was reading. Six hours later, it's three in the morning and I'm racing through the last few chapters, unable to sleep until I know how it all ends. Set in an idyllic small town rooted in family history and horrific secrets, *Bloodline* is *Pleasantville* meets *Rosemary's Baby*. A deeply unsettling, darkly unnerving, and utterly compelling novel, this book chilled me to the core, and I loved every bit of it."

—Jennifer Hillier, author of *Little Secrets* and the award-winning *Jar of Hearts*

"Jess Lourey writes small-town Minnesota like Stephen King writes small-town Maine. *Bloodline* is a tremendous book with a heart and a hacksaw . . . and I loved every second of it."

—Rachel Howzell Hall, author of the critically acclaimed novels *And Now She's Gone* and *They All Fall Down*

PRAISE FOR *UNSPEAKABLE THINGS*

Winner of the 2021 Anthony Award for Best Paperback Original

Short-listed for the 2021 Edgar Awards and 2020 Goodreads Choice Awards

"The suspense never wavers in this page-turner."

—*Publishers Weekly*

"The atmospheric suspense novel is haunting because it's narrated from the point of view of a thirteen-year-old, an age that should be more innocent but often isn't. Even more chilling, it's based on real-life incidents. Lourey may be known for comic capers (*March of Crimes*), but this tense novel combines the best of a coming-of-age story with suspense and an unforgettable young narrator."

—*Library Journal* (starred review)

"Part suspense, part coming-of-age, Jess Lourey's *Unspeakable Things* is a story of creeping dread, about childhood when you know the monster under your bed is real. A novel that clings to you long after the last page."

—Lori Rader-Day, Edgar Award–nominated author of *Under a Dark Sky*

"A noose of a novel that tightens by inches. The squirming tension comes from every direction—including the ones that are supposed to be safe. I felt complicit as I read, as if at any moment I stopped I would be abandoning Cassie, alone, in the dark, straining to listen and fearing to hear."

—Marcus Sakey, bestselling author of *Brilliance*

"*Unspeakable Things* is an absolutely riveting novel about the poisonous secrets buried deep in towns and families. Jess Lourey has created a story that will chill you to the bone and a main character who will break your heart wide open."

—Lou Berney, Edgar Award–winning author of *November Road*

"Inspired by a true story, *Unspeakable Things* crackles with authenticity, humanity, and humor. The novel reminded me of *To Kill a Mockingbird* and *The Marsh King's Daughter*. Highly recommended."

—Mark Sullivan, bestselling author of *Beneath a Scarlet Sky*

"Jess Lourey does a masterful job building tension and dread, but her greatest asset in *Unspeakable Things* is Cassie—an arresting narrator you identify with, root for, and desperately want to protect. This is a book that will stick with you long after you've torn through it."

—Rob Hart, author of *The Warehouse*

"With *Unspeakable Things*, Jess Lourey has managed the near-impossible, crafting a mystery as harrowing as it is tender, as gut-wrenching as it is lyrical. There is real darkness here, a creeping, inescapable dread that more than once had me looking over my own shoulder. But at its heart beats the irrepressible—and irresistible—spirit of its . . . heroine, a young woman so bright and vital and brave she kept even the fiercest monsters at bay. This is a book that will stay with me for a long time."

—Elizabeth Little, *Los Angeles Times* bestselling author of *Dear Daughter* and *Pretty as a Picture*

PRAISE FOR *THE CATALAIN BOOK OF SECRETS*

"Life-affirming, thought-provoking, heartwarming, it's one of those books that—if you happen to read it exactly when you need to—will heal your wounds as you turn the pages."
—Catriona McPherson, Agatha, Anthony, Macavity, and Bruce Alexander Award–winning author

"Prolific mystery writer Lourey tells of a matriarchal clan of witches joining forces against age-old evil . . . The novel is tightly plotted, and Lourey shines when depicting relationships—romantic ones as well as tangled links between Catalains . . . Lourey emphasizes the ties that bind in spite of secrets and resentment."
—*Kirkus Reviews*

"Lourey expertly concocts a Gothic fusion of long-held secrets, melancholy, and resolve . . . Exquisitely written in naturally flowing, expressive language, the book delves into the special relationships between sisters, and mothers and daughters."
—*Publishers Weekly*

PRAISE FOR *SALEM'S CIPHER*

"A fast-paced, sometimes brutal thriller reminiscent of Dan Brown's *The Da Vinci Code*."
—*Booklist* (starred review)

"A hair-raising thrill ride."

—*Library Journal* (starred review)

"The fascinating historical information combined with a storyline ripped from the headlines will hook conspiracy theorists and action addicts alike."

—*Kirkus Reviews*

"Fans of *The Da Vinci Code* are going to love this book . . . One of my favorite reads of 2016."

—*Crimespree Magazine*

"This suspenseful tale has something for absolutely everyone to enjoy."
—*Suspense Magazine*

PRAISE FOR *MERCY'S CHASE*

"An immersive voice, an intriguing story, a wonderful character—highly recommended!"

—Lee Child, #1 *New York Times* bestselling author

"Both a sweeping adventure and race-against-time thriller, *Mercy's Chase* is fascinating, fierce, and brimming with heart—just like its heroine, Salem Wiley."

—Meg Gardiner, author of *Into the Black Nowhere*

"Action-packed, great writing taut with suspense, an appealing main character to root for—who could ask for anything more?"

—Buried Under Books

PRAISE FOR *REWRITE YOUR LIFE: DISCOVER YOUR TRUTH THROUGH THE HEALING POWER OF FICTION*

"Interweaving practical advice with stories and insights garnered in her own writing journey, Jessica Lourey offers a step-by-step guide for writers struggling to create fiction from their life experiences. But this book isn't just about writing. It's also about the power of stories to transform those who write them. I know of no other guide that delivers on its promise with such honesty, simplicity, and beauty."

—William Kent Krueger, *New York Times* bestselling author of the Cork O'Connor series and *Ordinary Grace*

JUNE BUG

OTHER TITLES BY JESS LOUREY

MURDER BY MONTH MYSTERIES

May Day

June Bug

Knee High by the Fourth of July

August Moon

September Mourn

October Fest

November Hunt

December Dread

January Thaw

February Fever

March of Crimes

April Fools

STEINBECK AND REED THRILLERS

The Taken Ones

The Reaping

THRILLERS

The Quarry Girls

Litani

Bloodline

Unspeakable Things

SALEM'S CIPHER THRILLERS

Salem's Cipher

Mercy's Chase

GOTHIC SUSPENSE

The Catalain Book of Secrets

Seven Daughters

CHILDREN'S BOOKS

Leave My Book Alone! Starring Claudette, a Dragon with Control Issues

YOUNG ADULT

A Whisper of Poison

NONFICTION

Rewrite Your Life: Discover Your Truth Through the Healing Power of Fiction

JUNE BUG

JESS LOUREY

THOMAS & MERCER

Text copyright © 2007, 2018, 2024 by Jess Lourey
All rights reserved.

Published by Thomas & Mercer, Seattle

www.apub.com

Amazon, the Amazon logo, and Thomas & Mercer are trademarks of Amazon.com, Inc., or its affiliates.

ISBN-13: 9781662519253 (paperback)
ISBN-13: 9781662519246 (digital)

Cover design and illustration by Sarah Horgan

Printed in the United States of America

JUNE BUG

Chapter 1

In my dream, I stumbled days and nights through the woods to reach the clear, burbling creek. A tower built to look like a silo loomed at the water's edge, and I knew I was home. The full moon shone while the frog sounds of night sang to me. When I lay on the edge of the creek to rest, I was suffused with serenity. A warm breath on the back of my neck and a hand on my shoulder comforted me. I felt protected, covered in cozy warmth.

But then the hand crept purposefully lower.

Then I smelled digesting Schlitz on the tepid breath.

I wasn't in paradise anymore.

My body lurched awake, and I was on my feet before I even remembered I'd been lying down. The vertigo caught up with me, and I clutched at a bedpost, blinking rapidly, my heart throttling around in my chest.

"What!" I yelled.

"Sunny?" slurred the voice in my bed.

I shook my head, and some REM-spun cobwebs fell out. I wasn't in my apartment in Minneapolis, where I'd lived for nearly ten years—a second-story complex on the West Bank where I'd lived alongside a sexy, blue-eyed saxophone player in his sixties and a compulsively clean law student. I'd moved out in April, leaving behind Bad Brad, my cheating boyfriend, as well as my career as an overeducated, over-partying waitress. I'd been housesitting for my friend Sunny ever since, living in her double-wide on the outskirts of Battle Lake, Minnesota, three hours northwest of the Cities.

And there was a strange man in her bed.

Make that *my* bed.

I flicked on the cat-shaped lamp and angled the lit ears toward the intruder sprawled on top of the red-and-blue Amish quilt I'd lucked into at the Fergus Falls Salvation Army. I yanked the blanket from under him and used it to cover my summer pajamas—an oversize, threadbare white tank top. I was comfortable with my five-foot-six, 140-pound frame, but I was no flasher. I shoved my disheveled hair away from my face and stared down my nose at the relaxed drunk, his back to me.

"Sunny isn't here." I was hoping to conjure a verbal vanishing potion, but my heart was still pummeling my rib cage, and my voice shook. Sunny's dog, Luna, now my foster dog, was barking frantically outside the open window, sensing my distress. "Who the hell are you?"

"Mira?"

Luna's barking ceased.

I squinted. Happy Hands knew me, and Luna knew him. His voice scratched an itch in the back of my memory. "Jason?"

"Yeah." He stretched. "You're not Sunny." He sounded bored.

Yup, it was Jason. I'd first met him through my moody friend Cecilia ten years earlier, when my hair was dyed black, I smoked clove cigarettes, and dark, flowing clothes had been my signature. Thank god for evolution.

Back then, Cecilia and I were both awed first-years trying to act like we weren't scared by the vastness of the U of M and its forty-thousand-plus students. We'd ended up as dorm mates through the luck of the draw, two small-town girls overwhelmed by the big city. We hit it off from the word go, to the point that I went to her hometown rather than mine during our first holiday break.

During that initial introduction to Battle Lake, I'd met Sunny, one of Cecilia's close friends. I'd also crossed paths with Jason Blunt, their high school classmate. He'd shown up at a lot of the subsequent parties

Cecilia and I road-tripped to, but he and I never really connected. He was the guy always trying to get in everyone's pants, the one who'd propose marriage to anyone smart enough not to sleep with him.

He was tall, over six feet, with dark hair and dark eyes, cute in a way that'd be hot if he were an actor but that ended up just average since he was a perpetually horny fiber-optic cable layer. In small-town tradition, Sunny and Jason had slept together in high school, as had most of their friends.

Musical beds, a game born of long winters and bad TV reception.

I hadn't seen Jason in more than five years. Word was he'd had to relocate to Texas to find someone to marry since every woman in Minnesota had turned him down. He clearly hadn't gotten the news that Sunny had moved to Alaska for the summer, and he was here making his local horn call.

"What're you doing back in Battle Lake?" I asked.

I felt lightheaded. It occurred to me that maybe Otter Tail County had some sort of magnetic pull on people. That was the only way to explain why I was still here, running the library and writing for the local newspaper after the May I'd survived. It's a long story, but here's the short version: I'd just started falling for a guy—a smart, funny, cute archaeologist with magic hands—when I found him shot through the head.

It ripped out my heart.

After he was murdered and his corpse left for me to find in the library, I learned again the battery-acid truth that my depth of attachment to another person had no effect on whether they got to live. I thought I'd internalized that one well enough when my dad died while drunk driving the summer of my junior year, but in my experience, life kept dragging you back to the same buffet until you picked the right food.

I'd also turned twenty-nine in May, but that milestone got lost in the rubble.

Jason sat up and rubbed a red scrape on his shoulder, his back still to me. He'd put on about forty pounds since I last saw him, and I couldn't help but notice that he'd stripped down to his ratty gray boxers. Confident guy.

"I'm in town to visit the 'rents. Got anything to eat?"

My mouth opened in a yell, but he was out of bed and stumbling toward the kitchen before I could answer. Apparently, if he wasn't getting laid, he was getting fed. I squelched the urge to hand him a mirror. I'd just watched a Nature Channel show on chimpanzee behavior and was pretty sure the shiny glass would keep him busy for hours.

No, better to feed him and send him on his way. It wasn't his fault I wasn't Sunny.

I stopped midway through grabbing for my robe, realizing what I'd just done: made excuses for his poor behavior when I should have instead kicked the trespassing horndog out on his ass. *Frack.* I finished pulling on the satin robe, cursing myself as I tied the sash. Knowledge hadn't set me free. I was going to play nice and hope he left quietly.

Score one for cultural conditioning.

I scanned the bedroom for a pair of shorts to put on under the robe. I grabbed the quilt off the floor and tossed it on top of the wrought iron bed, discovering the cutoffs I'd been wearing earlier beneath. I tugged them on.

Now that I was no longer on red alert, I couldn't ignore the black memory squirming up through my sea of consciousness. I didn't want to acknowledge it, but no way could I sit on it any longer, not now that we were bathed in light and I could hear Jason making himself comfortable in my kitchen.

It'd happened nearly a decade earlier, the summer before Cecilia and I graduated from college. The night had opened with promise—a bonfire by the lake, a keg of Leinenkugel's, and a CD player hooked up to someone's car lighter. I remember feeling pretty that night, excited to be with friends.

Jason was there, and it wasn't long before he hit on me. His hair was longer then, shiny black and tucked into a man-bun at the base of his neck. When he leaned in to tell me a joke, his wide grin was flirtatious. I was flattered by the attention but not drunk enough to latch on to the token male slut so early in the evening. When I didn't bite, he moved on to the next chick, and I forgot about him.

He hadn't forgotten about me.

When I walked into the woods to pee, he followed, not making a sound. He waited until my pants were down to push me onto the ground and cover my mouth with his palm. His hand smelled musty, like composting leaves. My brain went white with terror.

That's when Sunny called my name. She staggered through the trees, and he jumped off me. She was weaving and giggling like we were playing hide-and-seek and didn't stop him when he shoved past her. Though she helped clean me off, she didn't have much sympathy for my situation. She wanted to keep the good times rolling and claimed Jason was just being drunk and stupid. She seemed mildly offended that I'd even consider that her good friend could be a potential rapist.

I started to wonder if maybe I'd overreacted.

Later that night they were laughing together as I sat on the fringes and tried to act normal, chain-smoking as I replayed the brief event over and over in my head. It couldn't have lasted more than three seconds. That wasn't that long, right? One, two, three. Maybe it was nothing. But I couldn't stop smoking and shaking.

In the way of small-town, stoic Scandinavian descendants, however, we never talked about that ugly night again. Life went on, and when I next ran into Jason at Cecilia's graduation party, he was distant and vaguely unpleasant. Everyone else treated him like a lovable goofball, though I noticed that some people made a point to steer clear of him.

So I buried the memory in my graveyard, when it should have gone in his.

Now that it'd surfaced, though, it was impossible to feel comfortable with him in my house. But I didn't want to work myself into a panic attack, either. I rationalized that plenty of people liked Jason, and he *did* have a good sense of humor. I stopped just short of making excuses for his past behavior and strode purposefully into the kitchen.

"So, I bet your parents are happy to see you." When I realized I was tracing infinity symbols on my thumbnails, I shoved my hands into my robe pockets to hide the nervous habit.

"Haven't been there yet." He grabbed a pot from the particleboard cupboard and stuck his hand in the food cabinet all in one smooth move. "You're gonna need more Potato Buds."

I sucked in a deep mouthful of air in a trapped sort of way and dropped onto a stool next to the island, girding myself for a confrontation. I knew from experience that it'd be easier to get rid of him on a full stomach rather than kick him out hungry, so I promised myself I would show him the door as soon as he was done eating.

This was my house, and I wasn't going to let him intimidate me in it.

At least not for longer than half an hour.

I calmed my nerves by making a mental note of the objects within reach that I could use as weapons—the knife rack stood inches away, and I could grab the nearest lamp in less than a second. Luna whined at the door, and I walked over to let her in. Jason must have locked her doggy door when he arrived.

Luna padded in eagerly, and I let the screen door close behind her. The June night was unusually warm, following May's precedent. The air was soaked in the smell of fresh-cut grass. If I listened below the kitchen sounds of boiling water and clattering pans, I could hear mosquitoes whining.

Whiskey Lake's waves lapped against the rim of its sheltered bay eight hundred yards from my front door. The oaks and elms skirting it stood still as stone, their fresh leaves hanging motionless. I cocked my head.

If there was no wind, there should be no waves.

I angled my ear toward the screen. Sure enough, I caught the low hum of a motorboat. I glanced at the clock hung by the door.

It was 2:34 a.m.

"What's a boat doing out at this time of night, and with no lights on?" I whispered, my fingertips on the cool screen.

I jumped as Jason answered from directly behind me. "Probably looking for the diamond. The lake'll be crawling by tomorrow."

Chapter 2

When Sunny's parents had disappeared nearly twenty years earlier, she'd automatically inherited their property. It came to a little more than a hundred acres of the prettiest land in Minnesota, with a sky-blue farmhouse, a barn, and three red sheds planted in the center of it. When the house burned down last year due to an electrical fire, Sunny replaced it with a double-wide. Surprisingly, it hadn't affected the charm. There were still rolling hills, tillable farmland, and wild prairie freckled with thick hardwood groves, plus the property's jewel: the lakeshore. Sunny owned the north side of Whiskey Lake from the public-access boat landing to her little private beach.

The only gap in her empire was the jutting peninsula known as Shangri-La. It shared the two-mile driveway that abutted Sunny's farm, its length of road leading to a waterlocked thumb of land on which rested the Shangri-La Resort. The dwellings—a beautiful main lodge and four cabins for the help—had been built in 1924 by Philadelphia millionaire Randolph Addams and his wife, Beatrice Carnegie, granddaughter of Phillip Carnegie. Addams had fallen in love with the area on a fishing trip and hired local workers to build the main structure out of fieldstone and cedar. Local legend had it that one summer a wealthy guest of the Addamses' had gone swimming wearing a diamond necklace. She emerged from the water without it. The other guests and staff had searched frantically.

The jewel, a diamond reportedly the size of a baby's fist, was never found.

Time passed. People forgot about it.

But according to Jason, that had suddenly and dramatically changed. A national travel magazine had published an article on what was now Shangri-La Resort. The piece mentioned the missing diamond, and one of the many people who read the article happened to be a Saint Paul *Pioneer Press* reporter. She had family in the Battle Lake area and thought the missing diamond necklace would make a terrific human-interest story.

The front-page headline of Friday's Source section read, Hope for a Diamond in Minnesota's Gorgeous Lake Country. The paper would be planting an imitation necklace in a weighted box in Whiskey Lake on Monday, and they were offering $5,000 and a free week at Shangri-La to whoever discovered it. Either they didn't have complete faith in the legend of the real diamond or, if they did, had decided it was beyond recovery. But the article made good copy and was a boon for the tourist industry that drove Minnesota summers.

Unfortunately, the paper had not seen fit to warn either the local papers or the Battle Lake residents. Here I was, Mira James, star reporter (well, reporter) for the *Battle Lake Recall* and living on the very shores of Whiskey Lake, and I had to get the scoop from a guy who liked ketchup and Easy Cheese on his rehydrated mashed potatoes. Technically, it was Sunday morning, which meant the contest started tomorrow.

"How'd *you* hear about it?" I asked peevishly.

Jason took a chug off the Dr Pepper he'd found in the back of the fridge and burped. His brown eyes traveled around the room, annoyed or distracted. He hadn't even considered a smile since he'd arrived, so I couldn't see if he still had those brace-straightened whites that made hearts flutter.

Until a person got to know him, that was.

"Word gets around." He turned to grab his shirt. He'd folded it in a pile with his pants and dock shoes outside my bedroom door, next to a flashlight and a six-pack of cheap beer.

"All the way to Texas?" I pressed.

His shoulder blades tensed. Although he hadn't minded talking about the diamond between shovelfuls of Potato Buds, when it came to discussing his life, he wasn't forthcoming. He rubbed the scratch on his back again, this time with more intensity. In the light, it looked angry and infected, with two shallower scrapes running parallel to it. I wondered if he was getting cat scratch fever. The kind you get from getting scratched by a really big cat.

"I left Texas a while ago," he said. "I was working up on the East Coast."

"Doing what?" My fingers were still tracing infinity shapes. I ran my hand through my shoulder-length brown hair and forced my body to be still.

"Working." He pulled his shirt sharply over his head, covering the scrapes. Suddenly, he couldn't leave fast enough.

"Mm-hmm." Just like that, the power in the room had shifted. I blinked at him, much like a pit bull did when it sensed it should probably let go of the person in its mouth but couldn't remember how to unlock its jaw. "What kind of work?"

He stopped in midtuck and turned toward the door. "Construction."

"House or road?"

"Jesus, Mira, back off!"

My neck twitched. If I was reading this situation correctly, Sunny's house had been Jason's first stop. If he were really in town to see his parents, then he would've stayed there. Horny or not, he was still a born-and-bred Minnesota Lutheran boy, and he knew he'd never hear the end of it if he came here first.

No, there had to be more incentive to pull Jason over Sunny's way than the promise of Potato Buds and tuna surprise. The *Pioneer Press* contest was the obvious reason, but how *had* he found out about it? He'd dodged the question. He didn't have a reputation as much of a reader, so it was unlikely he'd been perusing a travel magazine or the newspaper's online version. And since no one in the Battle Lake area yet knew about the diamond search—because if they had, it would have gotten back to the *Recall*, given the momentum theory of small-town rumors—it was even less likely that someone from here had contacted him.

He was almost out the door, but I suddenly wanted him to stay and answer my questions.

Jason had other plans. He was fully dressed, his clenched jaw furrowing a shadow from his temple to his mouth. He shoved past me, flashlight and beer in hand. His elbow connected with mine in a sharp crack, and I couldn't tell if it was intentional. At the door, he turned and glanced once into my eyes, his dark brown staring down my gray. The rage in his made me shiver. And then the screen door slapped closed and I was left alone with a crusty potato-making pan, a counter full of open condiments, and the feeling that Jason and I would be seeing each other again real soon.

I wiped my nose and began cleaning up, not relaxing until his taillights disappeared. My hands were shaky, and I felt displaced and edgy. I knew one thing that would calm me down, but I didn't like to give in to the bad habit.

I paced the kitchen, still thick with the smell of fake potatoes and Jason's spicy-cheap Drakkar cologne, and listed all the reasons it would be a bad idea to rip into my old standby:

- Although it made me feel good for the moment, coming down was always hard.
- Empty calories at night go straight to the designated ass pockets.
- I'd need to brush my teeth again.

Screw it.

I walked to the freezer and yanked out a red-and-green Nut Goodie package quickly, before reason or good sense took over.

Frozen Nut Goodies were the only way to go in the summer. The cool chocolate slid around on your tongue, and the maple center got hard and chewy all at once, like iced-up honey. I peeled the wrapper and bit off the chocolate lip, letting the sweet darkness and nuts merge. When I reached the light-brown maple center, I was forced to leverage the bar between my molars to crack off a piece. I braced a chunk and sucked it slowly, letting the crystallized, nutty sugar dissolve into my veins. I felt a spreading warmth as I settled into my Nut Goodie high, the world and all its creatures right for one perfect moment.

"Hey, Luna. Wild night, eh?" I scratched behind her ears. She was a German shepherd mix that Sunny had found on the side of Highway 210 when she was only a floofball puppy. When I took over as house sitter, Luna was part of the package. She got along fine with Tiger Pop, my calico kitty and consummate coward. I hadn't seen her since Jason arrived, and my best guess was that she was sleeping in her second favorite spot in the house—the pile of clean clothes in the laundry room.

It was 3:23 Sunday morning by the time the kitchen was back in order, and a focused to-do list buzzed in my head: stop the presses and submit an article for Monday's *Recall* ASAP so we didn't look like dorks, ask around about Jason to satisfy my curiosity, research the tale of Whiskey Lake and the real diamond necklace, and reclaim my feeling of safety.

Oh, and rent some diving equipment while there was still some to be had.

Chapter 3

The fresh, metallic tang of ink washed over me as I entered the *Battle Lake Recall* office. Except for the smell, the two-room rented space could pass for a DMV waiting area. The walls and carpeting were an institutional beige, no art hung on the walls, and the only furniture was gray metal filing cabinets and a desk, which was where I found Ron seated.

It took me all of thirty seconds to fill him in.

"Hell on fire," he said, rubbing his face. "When did the *Pioneer Press* article come out?"

Ron was the *Recall's* owner, editor in chief, desktop publisher, full-time reporter, photographer, and salesman, which was why he was in the office early on a Sunday. He was a mostly harmless guy in his late forties with thinning gray hair who usually wore tan clothes. Come to think of it, he was the human version of his office.

His main claim to fame other than the newspaper was his excessive public displays of affection with his wife, Rhoda. They did everything short of lift their legs and spray each other. The two of them had gotten kicked out of a bar or two for their extreme PDA, but mostly everybody in town was just happy to see married people making out with the people they'd married.

Ron had originally hired me on to write fill-in articles, though he'd given me more work since May, including my very own recipe column, called Battle Lake Bites. My weekly goal was to find a gastronomic combination that, in Ron's words, "was representative of Battle Lake." So far, my two hits had been "Phony Abalone" (chicken soaked in clam juice so it tastes like fish) and "Deer Pie" (think Freddy Krueger meets Bambi topped with Velveeta).

Between me and Betty Orrinson, a lovely woman who wrote the Tittle-Tattler column, the *Recall* had a total of three employees. And unless Betty was holding out information, which would have been counterintuitive, not one of us had heard about the *Pioneer Press* article until it was almost too late. I'd dropped by the library to print out a copy of it, which I slapped on his desk. "The contest officially starts tomorrow at dawn, but there were already boats out on Whiskey at two thirty this morning."

Ron leaned back in his swivel chair, crossed his legs, and hoisted them onto his desk with a grunt, lacing his fingers behind his head. I imagine he was going for a Woodward and Bernstein pose of urgent journalistic thought, but the gap in his shirt above the top snap of his pants leaked out too much belly-button hair for that.

"Blessed big-city newspapers. Think they don't need to inform the little guy what's going down in his very own town. Well, this little guy has a trump card: the human-interest angle. You know Shirly Tolverson, down at the Senior Sunset?"

I hadn't been around long enough to know all the locals by name, but I certainly knew the Senior Sunset. In fact, I was becoming a little too familiar with it. I'd spent a lot of time there last month trying to figure out who'd killed my archaeologist lover.

Most of the Sunset folks were great, and a few of them were emerging as friends. I'd gone back just last week to help till and plant their little rectangle of garden, staying to play three-handed Schafkopf with some residents. I left $4.75 poorer and convinced I'd spend more time there if not for the smell. It was the perfume of a small-town prom gone bad—cafeteria food, drugstore makeup, and Lysol.

"I know my way around the Sunset," I told Ron, "so I'm sure I could track her down."

"Him. Shirly's dad sold the lumber to the Addamses to build Shangri-La, and Shirly helped out when he was a kid. I used to hear him tell tales of it at the Turtle Stew. Go see him pronto and find an angle. I'll pull the layout and make room." Ron dropped his legs to the floor and rested his elbows on his desk, a rare look of purpose in his eyes. "You email me an article before midnight tonight. Damn good thing this paper comes out on a Monday, or we'd be caught hanging in the wind with our pants down."

A 40-watt bulb switched on over Ron's head, and I wondered if his "pants down" comment had given him an idea of something new to try with Rhoda. I hurried out, overhearing him mutter about the "fishing contest on the back page" and "teed-off Lutherans." He could complain about the hassle of rearranging the layout on a paper ready to go to press, but I think he was pleased to have a sense of urgency. That had to be why people went into journalism: to feel like they were breaking important news and helping people. At the *Recall,* the majority of our reporting dealt with high school sports, who'd gotten arrested for what, and which kids had gotten scholarships to where.

I stepped out into the cloudy June day and glanced at my watch—10:33. Probably nearing snack time at the Sunset, but if I beat cheeks the four blocks, I could be there and gone before the meal was served. I wasn't sure what a room full of geriatric diners looked like, but I was willing to bet the sound stuck with a person for a while.

I was passing First National Bank when a barn swallow swooped down from its nest in the bank clock and dived at my head. I squealed and dropped to the sidewalk, heart racing. Being swooped at was a terrible omen! I kept my feeders full to appease the avian gods—I was legitimately terrified of birds, which were really just flying lizards—but despite my best efforts, this barn swallow had come to curse me. Did it have something to do with me bringing Tiger Pop along when I moved here? Or maybe the water in the bird bath outside the double-wide was stale.

"Mira? You sure are up early on a Sunday."

Aw crap. That's what the swallow had been up to, warning me that Kennie Rogers, Battle Lake mayor and resident busybody, was coming around the corner. Maybe I'd need to rethink my view of birds.

"Hi, Kennie." I stood, gingerly wiping my knees. "Actually, I'm usually up—"

"And did you get your hair cut? It's so flattering, that field-worker look. So natural. I wish I could pull it off." Kennie beamed at me, smoothing her frayed denim vest with her free hand. She must have greased the inside to squeeze into it, because her boobs were squished together into an enormous uni-breast with barely a crack in the top. Her hair was frosted perfection, the curled ends crackling with Aqua Net. One errant spark and she'd go off like a rocket. Her makeup was applied with its usual putty-knife precision, her eyelids a glittery purple underneath the penciled black brows, dark lines of blush along each side of her nose to make it look thinner, her lips a bruised raspberry with a brown pencil line tracing a perfect pout well outside her mouth's natural borders.

She was wearing rolled-up, faded Levi's and cork-heeled pumps, à la Jennifer Lopez, but instead of looking like a trendy Latina, Kennie managed to pass for a stuffed Norwegian. "Well, don't just stand there gaping," she said. "Aren't you gonna ask me what's in my hand?" She waved a stack of papers.

"What's in your hand, Kennie?" I asked, remembering that you're supposed to play dead when a charging animal comes at you. Or wait. Were you supposed to run?

"Flyers for my new business!" Kennie cried out. "Whee!"

Her last business had been old-lady beauty contests where there were no winners, if you know what I mean. That one hadn't even gotten off the ground. Before that, it had been a private, clothing-optional nightclub. I waved over Kennie's shoulder at an imaginary friend and took off jogging.

She chased after me, quick as a cheetah in her strappy sandals, and grabbed my arm. "You silly! Just take a peek. It doesn't cost a thing to look." She flashed me a sly smile.

I searched for help, but church was in session and the streets were empty. I was on my own, and my quickest route out of here was to take my medicine. I held out my hand. "Fine. Let's see it."

She eagerly thrust a brochure toward me.

It looked like it had been produced with the cheap desktop publishing software that came installed on most new computers nowadays. The paper was résumé thickness, tri-folded to create a pamphlet. On the front were two clip art suns, one next to the other, with the words "Minnesota Nice Inc." curved underneath like a grinning mouth. Held at arm's length, it resembled a New Age smiley face. I braced myself for wrinkly nudity of some sort and folded open the front flap, peering at it through one cracked eye.

"Well?" Kennie balanced impatiently on one foot while she fiddled with her cheap metal ankle bracelet.

I read the first paragraph—a bulleted list—out loud:

- Having trouble breaking up with that gal who doesn't let you watch football on Sundays?
- Struggling to let your fella know that either he learns to chew with his mouth closed or you start shopping for a new couch warmer?
- Can't kick that special someone off the funeral committee, even though NO ONE likes their five-meat hotdish?
- Don't want to tell Jimmy that he can't use your deer stand anymore because he's never gotten the hang of peeing out of a tree?

I shook my head in disbelief as I read on:

Then Minnesota Nice Inc. is for you! We do your dirty work. The truth shall set you free, and we'll tell it for a fee!

I laughed out loud. I couldn't help it. Kennie might finally be onto something. "So people hire you to tell the hard truth for them?"

She clapped her hands. "I *knew* you'd appreciate it. You and me are both intelligent women ready to face the new millennium. We know we gotta do for ourselves." She nudged me, hard, in the ribs, and yanked her brochure back. "I'll give you one of these when I get some more printed. I'm sure you'll let me put a whole pack out at the library. Right, sugar?"

Ah. The *actual* reason Kennie had stopped me in the street. She needed advertising real estate. "I suppose."

She smiled and waved her talons in my face, then turned on her five-inch cork heels and tottered away. I supposed a woman born, raised, and cured in Battle Lake who frequently pretended to have a southern accent should be expected to surprise, yet she'd caught me off guard once again. Minnesota Nice, indeed. I wished I'd written down the number. I wasn't a fan of confrontation.

Speaking of which, I hoped I could avoid one with the front desk people at the Senior Sunset. It was sometimes hard to slip past the security door, depending on who was working. It was just weird that the elderly had so little freedom. When they moved in, they had to sign a contract saying they wouldn't leave unsupervised, among other draconian rules. It turned the place into a jail with inmates who couldn't run to save their souls.

As I neared the Sunset's main door, I considered the turns of fate that had brought me here. Not so much "here" as in Battle Lake, but "here" at this point in my life. I'd fled my tiny hometown of Paynesville as soon as I graduated. I took off to Minneapolis, first moving into the U of M dorms before setting up base in my tiny West Bank apartment. After ten years in the city, though, I hadn't felt much more grounded or purposeful than I had in the horror known as high school. I'd been bopping around grad school, waiting tables, and hoping someone would bring meaning to my life.

I remember one particularly lost day, about five months before Sunny called to ask me to house-sit. I'd been trudging home from a late shift at the Vietnamese restaurant where I worked. It was an icy

November evening, and my coat was too thin. I'd forgotten to remove my required bow tie, which would get me in trouble at my next shift, and the thick smells of fish sauce and curry swarmed around my head like sluggish bees.

It was a couple hours before bar close, and I felt relatively safe. Even when I noticed the man walking across the Washington Avenue Bridge twenty paces behind me, I didn't think much of it. The streets were well lit, but out of an abundance of caution, I crossed to the other side of the bridge. He followed. I crossed back. He followed again. My apartment was two blocks away. I could see a clot of people laughing and hanging out outside Bullwinkle's, a local bar. I was so near to being enclosed in the warm light of their company.

I wasn't going to run. I was going to walk steadily.

My gloved hand felt for my keys deep in my pocket, and I laced one between each of my knuckles. I could hear the stalker coming closer, his breath matching mine, his feet crunching on the layers of ice frosting the sidewalk. The Bullwinkle's group was now only forty feet ahead. Traffic buzzed past, everyone safe in their cars.

Suddenly, the man grabbed my shoulder and twisted me around to face him. He wore a woolen cap pulled low over his face. He brushed up against me, something hard pressing into my side. I felt a hand inside my coat, and then a sharp tug at my shoulder, before he was gone, empty-handed. I didn't know if I had been molested, almost robbed, or hugged.

I stood there, mouth open, heart hammering.

It'd happened so fast that I hadn't taken my key-laced hand out of my pocket. I just watched him run away. Later that night, I lay in bed thinking about the existence I'd chosen for myself, in which I worked, slept, and drank, with only the occasional failed mugging to break up the monotony.

It hadn't felt good.

Fast-forward seven months, and here I was, in Hamm's land of sky-blue waters, one murdered lover under my belt and nearly a regular at the local nursing home. Was this life any better than the previous one?

I couldn't tell. I hoped so.

I stepped off the sidewalk and crossed the street onto the Sunset's land-scaped front lawn. This part of town was mostly residential, the houses small and boxy, built in the fifties. It was quiet except for the random ringing of church bells. When a breeze picked up, it carried the smell of fresh-baked bread from someone's open window.

I had just reached the Senior Sunset lobby doors when I heard a "Psst!" from the bushes.

I swiveled and spotted a fuzz of light gray and apricot on the other side of the yellow-flowered potentilla bush. "I can get you a pack of cigarettes, mint-flavored Maalox, or a pretty new crossword book," whispered the voice.

"Mrs. Berns?"

She was one of the younger residents, a spitfire who pretty much came and went as she pleased. My overriding hope in life was to be as much of a badass in my golden years as she was. And maybe to have her sex life. Mrs. Berns had more moves in one arthritic pinkie than I possessed in my whole body. She'd told me it took her an unfortunate marriage to figure out that she didn't need to buy the cow to get the milk, and she'd been burning through Battle Lake's geriatric singles scene ever since.

I peered behind the bush to see Mrs. Berns perched on a three-legged gardening stool, an inventory list in one hand and a short library pencil in the other. She'd dyed her hair since I'd last seen her, going from blue to light orange, the tightly permed curls covering her head like a steel-wool hat. Most of her face was lost behind a pair of enormous square-framed sunglasses.

"Did you just have eye surgery, Mrs. Berns?"

"Ssshh!" she hissed. "Whaddya need? Liquor? Bettie Page poster? Perry Como's Greatest Hits? You name it, I can get it."

As weird as it was, I had to admire the entrepreneurial spirit of this town's women. "I can buy all that stuff out here. I'm going *into* the nursing home. You should sell to the people on the inside, not the people on the outside."

She peered down at her check-free inventory list and back at the front door, and then back at her list. "Damn!" She grabbed her stool and whipped past me, leaving a faint smell of lemon verbena and pressed face powder.

I followed, a smile on my face. The Senior Sunset foyer was a cross between a dorm and a hospital. The floors were shiny faux-marble linoleum, and the walls were institutional green. The pictures hung on the walls looked like the work of a four-year-old with watercolors, all of them set in brass frames exactly five feet off the ground. I supposed the pastel colors were meant to soothe the residents into forgetting they were reasoning, functioning human beings. Thank all that's holy that Mrs. Berns was doing her part to keep the resistance alive.

The ceiling was covered with those squares of pocked tiles found in every high school in the country. They did wonders for the acoustics, which presently were being tested by a Muzak version of Blondie's "Rapture" piped out just loud enough to be annoying. I walked to the front desk like a woman in charge.

"What room is Shirly Tolverson in, please?" I could hear a faint weeping in the distance, and the bilious sound of Judge Judy on a bender coming from the community room television.

The man behind the counter wore janitorial overalls and held a mop in one hand and a phone to his ear with the other. "Yeah, down the hall, fifth door on the right." He waved me on and returned to his conversation.

I almost signed in before realizing that I might not be allowed to enter if I was still standing here when the receptionist, who must have been on break, returned. I really didn't have a legitimate reason to be at the Sunset, though I could have lied if necessary. I scurried down the hall and slipped into the fifth door. An elderly man lay on the bed, a carpentry book in one hand, *Jeopardy!* on TV, and a bowl of peanut M&M's within reach. I liked his priorities.

"Mr. Tolverson?"

He glanced over, tugging his trifocals farther down his nose. Unlike some residents of the home, who wore muted "convenience clothes," he was dressed in street attire—ironed khakis and a plain navy-blue T-shirt. His hair was a crisp white and thick as a dictionary. The brown of his eyes was watery but their focus sharp, and his lips showcased a smile of even white teeth. They were probably dentures, but who was I to judge? He was a hottie of an old guy.

"May I help you?"

"Mr. Tolverson, my name is Mira James. I'm a reporter at the *Battle Lake Recall*."

"Oh yes, of course. I read your article on Jeff Wilson. A true shame about him. What can I do for you?"

I considered embellishing my story so we didn't look so stupid at the *Recall*, but Shirly Tolverson didn't seem like a man to lie to. "Ron Sims sent me over. We got scooped by the *Pioneer Press*. They heard there was a diamond necklace lost a number of years ago in Whiskey Lake, and Ron thinks you might know something about it. I'm trying to write a human-interest angle on the same story."

Shirly set down his book, removed his wire-rimmed glasses, and rubbed his eyes. He sighed profoundly. "What caused the *Press*'s interest in the diamond?"

I studied him. The mention of the necklace hadn't piqued his curiosity; it had *tired* him. "A reporter with family in the area heard about it through a random travel article on Shangri-La Resort and got the paper to run a contest. The first person to find the decoy diamond they plant gets five grand. They don't think there's any hope of finding the original lost diamond, I don't think. It's mostly a marketing gimmick to increase their readership around here, I suspect."

Shirly got a distant look in his eyes and leaned back on his pillow. "Shangri-La, located in the Valley of the Blue Moon." The reference was lost on me, but I didn't want to seem stupid, so I nodded in what I hoped was a wise manner.

He glanced my direction, a little past my head and to the left. "Well, Mira James, pull up a chair and I'll tell you what I know. When I'm done, you can decide for yourself if the real diamond will ever be found."

Chapter 4

According to Shirly, one spring afternoon, Randolph Addams had saun-
tered into Tolverson's Lumber and told the senior Mr. Tolverson that he
wanted to build "a little cabin" down on Whiskey Lake. First, he bought
the peninsula and access to it from Sunny's great-grandfather. Next, he
brought in an architect. When it came time to build the main lodge,
he spared no expense. Otter Tail County fieldstone was used to craft
the foundation and fireplaces. Mr. Addams sent for Brazilian mahogany
beams all the way from South America. The window frames featured
out-swinging sashes, grooved and cut for both screens and shutters with
all the hardware concealed—quite a novelty at the time. The workers
finished the outside with stained cedar shakes.

Once the main structure was completed, the architect ordered
hand-cut, French stained glass for the doors leading from the large
living room to the wraparound porch. He also had a system of buzz-
ers installed that connected to the newly built servants' cottages and a
dumbwaiter set up so food could travel from the first-story kitchen to
the second-story rooms without being seen.

The Addamses hosted grand parties for their friends from the East
once Shangri-La was completed. Randolph Addams's associates would
stay in one of the main lodge's nine bedrooms and be catered to by
the servants. Most of the workers were live-ins, though Addams hired
Shirly to do lawn work and run odd errands for the household. He'd

been on the beach the day the diamond went into the lake, working as a towel boy.

"So you saw the woman lose the necklace?" I asked.

"In a manner of speaking." Shirly removed his glasses and rubbed his eyes. "I saw her stroll into the water with a diamond the size of a caramel around her neck. I saw her walk out of the water without it."

I blinked. "Are you being intentionally vague?"

"'Vague' isn't the word, Ms. James. Her necklace wasn't the first piece of jewelry to disappear that summer, though that damned necklace was the official end of Shangri-La's relaxed days. She put up quite a stink when she lost it—made us workers search on hands and knees in two feet of water for several days. She swore she was going to make Mr. Addams replace the necklace if we didn't find it." Shirly studied the back of his veined hands. "Tell the truth, I don't know if she didn't *plan* to lose that necklace."

I sat up straighter. "Why would she do that?"

"The woman who claimed to lose the necklace, Regina Krupps, married into an upper-crust New York family. Back then, it took a lot longer to cross the country, so you remembered when someone came from New York or California." He frowned. "Mrs. Krupps never seemed to have as much money as the other guests, and she acted angry about it. The day she lost her necklace, I was delivering firewood to Mr. and Mrs. Addams's second-floor bedroom, and I caught her in their closet. She was initially scared, and then ticked off when she saw it was only a servant."

"Was she stealing?"

"You'd think, except I got the impression that she was *hiding* something back there. A few hours later, she loses her necklace, and it's me who's searching for it. She made Mr. Addams fire me and some of the other help when we couldn't find it in the lake. She said we were a bunch of lazy thieves."

That chapped my hide. "If she'd claimed she'd lost it, why would she accuse you all of being thieves?"

Shirly raised an eyebrow. "My guess is we reminded her too much of herself, and she'd been looking for any excuse to get us fired. Rumor had it that she was dirt poor until she married Bradford Krupps. It wasn't but a couple months after she had us canned that Mr. and Mrs. Addams sold the property, only a handful of years after they built it. They were sick of dealing with all the supposed thievery that was going on and all the police attention that came with it. Shangri-La's been a resort ever since."

I was looking at all the angles. "Was it a *real* diamond necklace that she lost?"

"She claimed it was."

He clearly didn't want to go on the record about that, but I got the impression the only real thing about that necklace was the bad luck it brought Shirly. I vowed to find out the whole story, even if I had to track down one of the original Addams family members.

Ha.

The Addams family.

Chapter 5

On my way out of Shirly's room, I considered how many years older than me he was because it might be time to become more open to dating outside my generation. I feared I was close to, if not immersed in, the relationship-atrophy phase of my life. It was a stage I'd seen coming for a while, a place in my personal evolution where if a guy hadn't gotten here with me, he'd be reluctant to leave the comfort of his train to jump on mine. Call it the "What do you *mean* you don't like peas in your macaroni and cheese?" point that we all reach, where we're simply too set in our ways to enter a healthy relationship with another person.

The threat of this specter was forcing me to consider new dating realms, though so soon after Jeff's death, I was officially hesitant about men. They had a lot to offer in theory, but in my experience, they tended to die too soon.

Starting with my father.

He'd been a career alcoholic too smart for his own good. My childhood was a tapestry of forced normalcy punctuated by raucous fights between my parents. By the time I was seven, I knew I couldn't have friends over because if my dad wasn't drunk, my mom would be yelling at him for being drunk the day before. I spent a lot of time in my room with my imaginary pals. It wasn't all bad—my family sometimes went on weekend camping trips, and when Dad was in public, he'd usually stay sober. Even drunk, he wasn't mean, just unstable. He believed, for example, that he could control the wind and speak French.

Apparently, both wind-talk and French shared a lot of root words with pig latin.

By my teen years, I'd learned how to shut down my emotions so as not to be a forced passenger on his roller coaster. I got even better at that after he died the spring of my junior year. He was driving drunk and slammed head-on into another car when he swerved over the center line. He killed himself and the other driver.

I finished growing up that day. I still wasn't sure if that meant I became an adult or a permanently stunted child.

Some days, I wasn't so sure there was a difference.

I was so lost in thought that I was on the other side of the security doors before I noticed the crowd gathered in the lobby. I had to stand on my tippy-toes to see what was going on. I was unprepared to find a lion tamer accompanied by a person of short stature wearing a lion costume at the center of the elderly mob.

"How about you, young lady?" boomed the lion tamer, beckoning to me dramatically. "Wouldn't you like to see a local production of the honorable William S. Shakespeare's *The Taming of the Shrew*, starring esteemed members of your community and played out in a Gothic carnival setting?"

I stepped back as he stepped forward and shoved a piece of paper into my hand. It was turning out to be a paper-shoving kind of day. This one was card stock with gilded letters in a flowing serif font proclaiming, *The Famed Romanov Traveling Theater Troupe Is Coming to YOUR Town!*

Underneath were pictures of the selfsame lion tamer, a Harlequin clown, comedy and tragedy, and various scantily clad women. It was like a Renaissance festival minus the big turkey legs and *Dungeons & Dragons* geeks. I wondered if Kennie was going to love this or hate it. I also wondered if the troupe knew the Senior Sunset folks were on lockdown. There was going to be no Gothic carnival for them, but I was intrigued.

"Sure," I said.

The tamer wore the wide, empty grin of somebody who smiles for a living. His nose was broad, and his eyes, small and close-set, darted around the room even as he talked at me. He seemed in habitual need of an audience. The lion wove in and out of the crowd, singing, dancing, and huzzahing, so I couldn't get a good look at him.

"'Sure,' it is! We are in agreement!" The lion tamer made a departing grand gesture with his plastic mini-whip and strode purposefully out the front doors of the Sunset, the lion man hurrying to catch up. I glanced around at the stunned room of nursing assistants and old folks they'd left in their wake.

A familiar face came forward, shaking his head. "And they call me crazy."

I smiled. "Hey, Curtis. How's the fishing?"

Curtis Poling was another of my faves at the raisin ranch. People said he was slow because he fished off the roof of the Sunset around lunchtime every day, despite the closest body of water being more than a mile away. I found Curtis to be wicked smart, though. He was also a hit with the ladies due to his ice-blue eyes and rakish charm.

"The fishing isn't great," he said. "I might need to switch bait."

I shook my head knowingly. "I recommend leeches."

Truth was, I knew nothing about fishing. In fact, I didn't even like to *eat* fish. I had an aversion to consuming anything that spent its whole life wet.

"Thanks for the tip," Curtis said, winking. "Don't be a stranger."

I watched him walk away, thinking that I'd just met my human-interaction quota for the day. It was time to rent a diving suit and tank to scope out Whiskey Lake's diamond graveyard.

Chapter 6

The aptly named Last Resort was the only place in all of Otter Tail County with scuba equipment for rent. The Resort was a standard Minnesota affair—small cabins facing water, a can of Off! in every kitchen, a dedicated fish-cleaning hut for all the vacationers to share.

Years ago, the owners, Sal and Bill Heike, had added scuba certification as a side business. They'd sunk a train car two hundred feet straight out from cabin number three. Unfortunately, pesticides and waste ponds around the lake had upset the water's delicate balance, and now the weeds were so thick on this side of the lake that visibility was only seven feet. The Heikes had to stop certifying divers but kept the equipment because used scuba gear didn't go for much. Bill also kept the tank filler, though he complained that it didn't pay, what with the cost of insurance.

I knew Bill and Sal from around town, mostly from their regular library trips to check out books on building your own greenhouse, making your own paper, growing your own organic vegetables, creating your own compost pile, et cetera. I also knew their twenty-two-year-old son, Jedediah. He'd tried to sell me pot on several occasions, and every time, he was genuinely astonished when I declined. The beauty of being a goof like Jed was that the world was born anew for you every day.

When I pulled my brown 1985 Toyota Corolla into the circle drive that marked the front of the Last Resort, it was Jed who limped out to greet me, his face lighting up when he saw it was me. "Hello, you!"

I smiled at his genuine happiness as I pulled myself out of the car. "What happened to your leg?"

Jed grinned sweetly, stretching the bong-shaped ring of acne around his mouth. "I twisted my knee unloading a boat yesterday. I am so all right, though. It's a beautiful day!" He waved his hands expansively in the air, the sun shining down on his curly light-brown hair and through the spindly Fu Manchu mustache he was trying to grow. He hugged me spontaneously, and I let him.

When he stepped back, still grinning, I returned his smile. He certainly made cluelessness look appealing. "Say," I said, "you wouldn't have any scuba equipment left to rent, would you?"

Jed actually scratched his head. "You know, weirdest thing. Everyone and her brother suddenly wants to rent our stuff. We're out."

My heart sank. I should have known. My ego liked the idea of breaking this story wide open, but it was the thought of winning five grand that really got me buzzing. I didn't have any house payments and my electric bill was currently low, leaving student loans as my only major expense—$276 every month. However, my part-time reporting job and now full-time library job paid only a frog's hair above minimum wage, which didn't leave a lot of spare cash lying around. It would have been nice to offer the $14.52 in my savings account some company.

"Well, 'cept for my stuff and Ma and Pa's. You could borrow that, if you like. We haven't been diving in a while."

"Jed!" I said delightedly. I was back on. "That would be great!"

He nodded like a happy Muppet and grabbed my hand. "Let's go check out the gear. It's all stored off the front office."

When we walked past the row of cabins, I noticed the Swenson's Nursery truck around the side of the Heikes' house. My heart took a little electric leap. Could it be? "Swenson's here doing some landscaping?"

"Yup."

"Who's doing the work?"

"Johnny."

My electric leap sparked into a full-grown power grid. I had a crush the size of a Mack truck on Johnny Leeson. He was tall, maybe six two; in his mid to late twenties; and had thick, longish blond hair. The Scandinavian-exchange-student look wasn't normally my type, but he was strong and lean, he had even white teeth, and he knew everything there was to know about gardening. When to plant your peas, how much water to give your corn, where to bury your tulip bulbs, how to fertilize your roses—if it could grow in dirt, Johnny could advise, and there was something erotic about a man with a green thumb. If he could coax blueberries to grow in low-alkaline soil, what could he do with a prematurely jaded woman on a Sealy pillow top? Plus, he always smelled like fresh-cut grass, and his eyes were the color of a blue raspberry slushie.

I was pretty sure he didn't know I had these lusty organic thoughts about him. He just saw me as the chick who bought a few seed packets every week. My crush felt safe and exciting at the same time. I reminded myself that I had no interest in dating, even if Johnny wasn't currently dating Liza, personal stylist at the Under the Lilacs salon in downtown Battle Lake.

"Where's Johnny now?" I said, my voice cracking slightly as I scanned the landscape.

"Dunno."

I tamped down a flicker of annoyance. It wasn't Jed's job to keep tabs on Johnny. "What's he working on here?"

Jed smiled. "Dunno."

By now we'd reached the resort office, and I didn't want to hurt Jed with any more probing. I'd simply need to roll with it if I saw Johnny. I ran my fingers through my hair to work through as many snarls as I could and followed Jed through the creaky door he held open. He'd brought me into a musty side porch. The mildewy smell reminded me of my grandma's basement, a dirt-floor affair where she kept her wringer washer and home-canned tomatoes. The Heikes' space was cluttered with cracked chairs stacked seat on seat, retired ice augers, and bright-orange, foamy flotation devices. Some old BCs—the buoyancy compensator vests that controlled a diver's depth and held the tank, air hoses, dive gauges, and regulator—and wet suits hung on ceiling hooks in a damp-looking corner.

He led me through the porch into the main office. It was surprisingly modern, with tongue-and-groove knotty pine walls, a sitting area with *In-Fisherman* magazines splayed around a Skittles-filled candy dish, and a long front counter. There was a newish Dell computer behind the desk hooked up to a scanner, printer, fax machine, and flat-screen monitor. I wondered how the Heikes could afford the new technology. It seemed like their resort was always half-empty since they'd had to close down the diving business, and they had no other income source that I was aware of. I thought the money would have been better spent on paint for the cabins, but maybe the computer saved time and helped them advertise.

"Just lemme check something real quick, and then I'll hook you up." Jed slid over the counter with a practiced air and grabbed one of the walkie-talkies near the computer. "Breaker, breaker, this is Angel Eyes, come in. Over." Jed winked at me and started getting the giggles.

"What is it, Jed?" Sal's voice was crackly.

"Heyah, Cool Mama, is cabin three still getting used tonight? Over."

Crackle. "No, Angel Eyes, cabin three canceled." Sal walked through the door, still speaking into the walkie-talkie. "They've moved to Shangri-La. Cool Mama out."

"Roger." Jed slid the walkie-talkie back into its holder, and Sal clicked hers off. She looked exactly like Jed, only thirty years older, silver threading her curls. "Hey, Mira," she said. "What brings you to our lonely resort?"

I frowned. I genuinely liked the Heikes. Being ex-hippies, they passed for diversity in greater Minnesota. "Business not so good, huh?"

"Not so good. But it'll pick up. We've got new plans."

I nodded at their computer. "You guys'll be fine. Anyhow, I'm just here to rent scuba equipment. I'm gonna do some diving on Whiskey."

"You and the rest of the county. What's going on over there?"

I considered not telling, but she was going to hear soon enough. I explained the missing-diamond story, the *Pioneer Press* drop box, and the $5,000 reward, adding, "I'm going to check it out. Who knows, maybe they dropped the box in early."

"Hmm. It might be time to pull me and Bill's gear out of retirement. Maybe we'll see you on the wet side, Mira!" Sal stepped over to the computer, clicked in a few words, and then exited through the back door. Jed followed her and was out of sight.

I knew he'd remember that I was waiting soon enough, so I poked my head out the nearest window. That's when I spotted Johnny next to the fish-cleaning shed, and my heart did a flutter tumble. The sun was kissing his rippling, sweat-glistened, shirtless body, and his thick hair curled around his ears and neck where it had gotten hot and wet. Except for the feed cap he wore where the olive leaf wreath should have been, he was Apollo soaking in the sun.

"Hey, Johnny, how's the day treating you?" I asked nonchalantly. And quietly. In my head. No way was I going to destroy this moment with my own brand of dorkism.

He was planting marigolds. I knew the flats of flowers he was unloading from the back of the pickup couldn't have weighed more than five pounds each, but when he grasped one, his arm muscles flexed and the lean ropes of his back defined themselves. His dark Levi's hung below the waist of his boxers, the whiteness of his underwear contrasting nicely with the brown muscles of his back. When he turned, I couldn't see his eyes behind his dark sunglasses, but his full lips were closed tightly as he concentrated on his work.

Once he had all the flats unloaded, he leaned over the side of the shed holding a garden spade. He dug down deeply, removing divots of earth, which he placed off to the side. Then he methodically and gently removed a marigold from its four-pack, placed it in the hole, held the earth clump over the flower, and shook the dirt loose from the sod. He repeated this for every flower. By the time he was halfway down the side of the shed, the hot sun was sending trickles of sweat down his back, through the soft valleys made by his lean hips, and into his promised land.

"Ready to go, Mira?"

I blushed and kept facing forward, thanking God almighty that a woman's hard-on was invisible. I shook my head to coax some blood back to my brain before I turned to look into Jed's friendly eyes.

"Oh, there's Johnny!" Jed pushed me aside. "Hey, Johnny, Mira's looking for you!" he yelled, waving and pointing over to where he'd pushed me, out of Johnny's view. "Here she is!" He held my hand out the window and waved it.

I peeked around the corner and smiled lamely. Johnny gave one brief wave, flashed a solemn smile, and strolled over, taking his gloves off as he walked with the self-assured grace of a panther.

"Hi, Mira."

I glanced at the blue toenail polish on my flip-flopped feet, certain that a movie reel of my impure thoughts was playing on the big screen above my head. Wait, that wouldn't work. I couldn't Rain Man my way out of this. I forced myself to make eye contact. "Hi, Johnny. What're you planting?"

He glanced back over his shoulder. "Marigolds, mostly. Have you gotten a chance to plant the zinnias you bought last week?"

My blush returned. He remembered I'd bought zinnias. Could it be that he thought about me as much as I thought about him? "Not yet. You've been too hot outside."

Johnny cocked his head. "Excuse me?"

My face burst into flame. "*It. It* has been too hot outside. To, you know, plant. Well, you better get to work, right? And I have to get to work. Not work, so much. More like investigating, you know. Underwater. I'm like a detective fish, but I can walk, too."

I swear to Athena I started jogging in place to demonstrate. In for a penny.

Johnny nodded, his expression quizzical, a small smile playing at the corners of his mouth. "Okay. Catch you later, you two."

35

Jed smiled dopily. Once Johnny was out of sight, I slid down the wall into a pit of shame. From that angle, I was able to flip my switch off Loser and onto Self-Loather. Could I *be* more of a moron? *I'm like a detective fish???*

But that man, that body, those gardening skills. I sighed. Johnny was off limits in real life, but I would have to seriously consider unpacking my vibrator out of homage to him. I'd retired it a few months earlier, concerned about overuse. It'd gotten to where I was having a Pavlovian response to the sound of any small electric motor. Even the buzz of a blender on liquefy could get me going.

After watching Johnny garden, though, one thing was clear: if I didn't take care of myself, I was going to do something silly like declare my love for the guy. "You got anything to drink, Jed?"

He peeked through the archway that led to the little resort store. "We have Coke. Or maybe you want to buy some pot?"

I tugged Jed toward the side porch. "Forget it. I gotta head. Which BC can I use?"

"That black one in back is mine." He pulled out one of the rickety chairs so he could reach the buoyancy compensator vest, tossing it over to me. Its hoses and gauges slapped around like octopus tentacles.

"This one's wet," I said, surprised. "I thought you three hadn't been diving for a while."

Jed opened his palms in a *who can remember everything?* way and hunted around for the rest of the gear. He ferreted out a wet suit, compass, diving knife, fins, mask, and snorkel, as well as a dive flag and an inner tube to strap the flag to so that all boats would know there was a diver down. Then he filled two air tanks and helped me haul them to my car. I was careful not to be caught ogling Johnny.

Again.

Once my Toyota was loaded, I avoided Jed's farewell hug for fear that I'd get sticky pheromones all over him. I couldn't resist asking one last question, though: "Is it expensive to get Johnny out to help landscape?"

Jed scratched his curly hair. "Not for us. He's doing it in trade for some work my dad did for his mom. If you want, I'll ask Johnny how much he charges."

"No!" I said, a little too loudly. Was it bad that, for a moment, I'd seriously considered hiring a hot garden man to gawk at from the comfort of the picnic table that served as my back porch? Probably, if only because I was broke.

One more reason to find the fake diamond.

I decided to put in at Sunny's little beach on the wide part of the road leading to Shangri-La. Her area was more grass than sand, but the lake out front was clear and hard-bottomed, and I was the only person with access here.

By now, Whiskey Lake was peppered with boats, even more than on a usual Sunday, and the public lake-access parking lot catawampus from Sunny's beach was nearly full. Most of the boats were concentrated on the east side of the lake, opposite Shangri-La. I wondered if they'd found something.

The BC was old but functional, and I had it attached to the tank in under four minutes. The wet suit and dive knife were easy to slip on, and a couple tugs set the face mask at the right pressure. I dragged the whole unit to the water so I could use the buoyancy of the vest to help ease the heavy tank onto my back.

Soon I was underwater, breathing in the silence of it.

Diamond hunting, here I come.

Chapter 7

Except for the Darth Vader sound of air leaving your mouthpiece, there was no perfect peace like scuba diving. It had the safety and coziness of a womb once your wet suit filled, the thin layer of water inside warmed by your body temperature. When you reached neutral buoyancy, the sensory deprivation elicited a sense of absolute freedom. I did a few horizontal twirls underwater, as I always do at the beginning of a dive, though I'd been diving only a dozen times in my life, and only once in the ocean.

My father had learned how to dive in the navy and taught me when I was ten. We'd traveled to Daytona Beach over Christmas. Dad talked a local dive shop into renting their gear even though Mom and I weren't certified with the promise that we'd stay close to shore. There was no coral off the beach and so nothing to see other than shady ocean, and it was butt-cold. Still, the attention from my dad felt good, even if we were shivering together in slate-gray, fish-free water. A couple years later, he sprang for me to get certified, and we dived some of the lakes around Paynesville. I think it was a way we could hang out together without needing to talk. As a bonus, he couldn't drink underwater.

After he died, it wasn't really something I could afford.

This time was a freebie, though, and I intended to enjoy it. I tried to sneak up on a few perch, but they muddied the water and darted away like mercury. My hands were glove-free because I liked to play them through the scratchy weeds and loose silt on the bottom. I was careful not to get tangled in the line to my inner tube, which was attached to the red-and-white flag marking my dive. With all the boats on the lake today, I needed to stay close to the tube. I didn't need an Evinrude outboard all up in my grill.

Once I acclimated to my environment, I settled in for some serious jewel hunting.

I eyeballed my compass, my plan to head generally southeast, which would land me in front of the Shangri-La main lodge. I swam steadily, using my feet to power me, my hands streamlined at my side. I skimmed just above the weeds, glancing occasionally at the treasure troves of Hamm's cans and severed anchors that sprouted like lake country anemones.

For the most part, Whiskey Lake was a pristine, spring-fed body of water with fifteen-foot-plus visibility on a good day, but even the cleanest lake carried the remnants of fishers past. Actually, Whiskey Lake was just what the locals called it; according to the DNR, who stocked it annually with walleye fingerlings and yearlings, the real name was Charter Lake. It was small, with a surface area of only 189 acres and a maximum depth of 46 feet. As a rule, I never went deeper than thirty feet when diving. It was too cold lower than that, though the bass, sunnies, and crappies that swarmed in the water without the DNR's help didn't seem to mind.

After a quarter of an hour underwater, I popped up to get my bearings. I was approximately forty feet from the Shangri-La beach, directly in front of it. *Perfect.* Surprisingly, there didn't seem to be any divers in the immediate vicinity, though I counted seven boats dotting the far side of the lake and a new group of divers ready to set off from the public access. Their diving flag slapped at the wind.

I sank slowly back down and continued to search. It's hard to distinguish one chunk of lake bottom from another, but I thought I could get a feel for the area so I'd know if anything had been changed or added. The *Pioneer Press* box wouldn't be planted until tomorrow sometime, according to their article, and I wanted to get the lay of the land before then. A flash of white caught my eyes, and I kicked down, my pulse quickening nicely. I checked my depth gauge. Twenty-three feet below the surface with more than half my air left. Was it a placeholder of some sort? A concrete box designed to hold the jewel, maybe? I grinned around my mouthpiece. Five grand would sure be nice to have. I could return to this spot first thing tomorrow and pluck the gem from the lake. An image of my dad smiling at me dropped unexpectedly into my brain, and with it, an even more surprising sensation of warmth. He'd be so tickled that something he taught me had paid off.

I kicked so mightily toward the white, already spending the money that I was sure I was setting myself up to find, that I almost had my face against it before I realized what it was.

A massive skeleton.

My hand flew to my dive knife as my throat constricted, causing me to suck in air through my nose. The indrawn breath suctioned the mask to my face and gave me a temporary feeling of suffocation, which set off a new round of anxiety. My head tossed left and right, trying to see everywhere at once, but the dive mask limited my peripheral vision.

I needed to calm the hell down. Panic while diving was deadly. My agitated movements were making my surroundings even murkier. I tried to still myself. I was safe. I was diving in a lake. There was all sorts of detritus down here, and so why not a skeleton? I hadn't been able to identify what kind of animal it was, but it was clearly not going to harm me. Besides, I could reach the surface in half a second by inflating my buoyancy compensator.

Repeating these thoughts allowed my pulse and the silt to settle. When my breath grew even, I floated back down for a closer look, shocked at the size of it. Its antlers told me it had been a full-grown moose, its bones laid cleanly on the lake bottom as it had drifted down in a final graceful ballet move to decompose peacefully. The moose must have fallen through the ice recently, probably this past winter, for the remains to be this pristine.

I filed away the skeleton as a good landmark for later and turned to swim back toward the beach. The water still had residual cloudiness from my little fit near the bones, so I sped up to reach a clearer spot.

It took only five strong kicks through the shadowy water until I was on top of the human body clad in the shark-gray wet suit, my tank tangled in the same rope that made and marked his grave.

Chapter 8

I fought and twisted at the rope like a hooked walleye, but the more I struggled to break free, the closer I brought myself to the body jerking on the other end like a rigid marionette. In one of my panicked gyrations, I saw the source of my present problem: a rock at the bottom of the lake, a yellow polypropylene rope tied securely around it and leading to the body floating ten feet below the surface. My oxygen tank was tangled on the rope.

But that visual information was quickly lost in the murk I was creating.

I couldn't fight the terror, made all the more poignant by the dead person who was almost on top of me now. My heart paused in my chest, building enough force to pound out my eardrums when it started again. I wrenched wildly to free myself, and the heavy, wet arm of the tangled corpse struck my head in a disjointed, dead swing, knocking off my face mask.

I blinked once, unseeing, only the rush of cold letting me know my eyes were open. The water was as final as gravedirt, and I sucked in a nose full of it as a fear reflex. I was now completely blind, dancing with a corpse, and drowning.

When I got scuba certified, my instructor spent half a day teaching us what to do if we lost our masks: stay calm, breathe through your mouthpiece, and slowly make your way to the surface. He hadn't covered what to do if we were also tangled in a rope tied to a rock and hooked to a dead body, but the principle was the same: don't lose your beans.

It was the only way to survive.

So even as I screamed for air and my lungs burned with water, I forced my raging fear instincts down and let the haunted corpse float right behind my unprotected neck. This allowed me to grab my BC vest buckles in a last-ditch effort to release myself and reach the surface. I wasn't deep enough to worry about the bends, even if I'd been thinking that clearly. For now, my brain was limited to one primal drive: get to the surface.

Now.

I unclasped the first buckle as white bursts of light flashed behind my eyes. I had the second one undone as everything began to go gray and my lungs blazed with the crushing weight of inhaled water. I'd been struggling too much, using too much oxygen. My cold fingers struggled with the last black clasp, finally freeing it. I kicked with all my remaining strength, blacking out even as I thrust forward.

I no longer knew which way was up. I was disoriented from the underwater fight with the rope and body, and I had no air bubbles in my lungs to release and guide me, even if I could see. I prayed that I was swimming toward the surface. If my head hit the soft bottom of the lake or just plowed through more water, I was dead. I wondered distantly if my dad would be waiting for me. He'd been dead for more than a decade, and I didn't know if I was ready to reconcile with him yet. With a few exceptions, he'd been a pretty selfish man when I knew him.

I realized the person I really wanted to see now was my mom, in real life. I'd always loved her but never trusted her because she'd let my dad do so much damage to all three of us. I figured a smart woman would have gotten us both out of there. His death pushed us even further apart. She certainly hadn't killed him, but she'd kept herself and me strapped to the kamikaze plane that was his life, which was why it was so hard to spend time with her after he died. Holiday visits, occasional letters or emails, all of them stiff and awkward, were our only contact.

That seemed so stupid now. I wished more than anything to be able to go for a walk with her, smelling the perfume of summer flowers, feeling the breeze in the sweaty hairs stuck to my neck, hearing gravel crunch underfoot. Instead, my world had narrowed to a tiny pinpoint of light. The tiny circle was growing brighter, but that couldn't be. My eyes were closed. Weren't they? Had I blacked out? Was I swimming toward the metaphorical light?

But the circle continued to grow larger until it became what looked like the sun reflected through a watery mirror. I reached out, and my hand brushed against something warm and soft. I grasped at it desperately, hungry to hold something solid. My hand slid off, so I dug my nails in and tried again, jerking myself up this time.

I was welcomed by the glory of the warm sun as I clutched at my inner tube. I hung on to the side and greedily sucked in air in between horking up lake water, grateful for the providence that'd brought me up near my life preserver. I didn't know if I'd have been able to swim much farther. My whole body was trembling, but my mind was rejoicing.

I was alive!

Chapter 9

I began to kick for the shore. I wanted to get as far away from that dead body and its watery grave as I could.

That could have been me.

The public access was closer than the little stretch of beach I'd started out on, and soon the diving crew I'd spotted earlier was beside me in their pontoon. I was dragged aboard, and I poured out my story between residual heaves. The dive crew untied their anchor, secured it to my inner tube as a marker, and took me ashore. They offered me an oversize Smurf beach towel and a canteen of stale drinking water. While we waited for the police, they told me they were from the Twin Cities, in Battle Lake to find the planted diamond. They'd been scoping out the area when they saw me pop to the surface and start puking.

As their lukewarm water scraped down my raw throat and I absorbed the hot sun of an early June afternoon, my stomach growled, reminding me I hadn't eaten anything all day. In hindsight, that was good. It wasn't long before the Battle Lake police were on the scene, and the county water patrol arrived shortly thereafter.

It was time to tell my tale again, this time to thirty-eight-year-old Battle Lake police chief Gary Wohnt. There was no love lost between Gary and me. The man knew I was always watching him out of the corner of my eye, and he returned the favor. He was thick necked and arrogant and had perpetually shiny lips. As a pure bonus, he had dark, inscrutable eyes and one of those ominously quiet personalities that forced me to fill the silence with embarrassing small talk and unrelated confessions.

Plus, he had a weird thing going with Kennie Rogers.

"Ms. James." His mirrored sunglasses reflected me back to myself, one of his hips cocked higher than the other, his meaty hands hanging loose at his sides.

"Chief Wohnt." I was sitting on the open rear of a diver's Mitsubishi pickup, the Smurf towel still held tight. Somebody had found me a Gatorade that tasted like flat soda and the color blue.

"Seems you were in the wrong place at the wrong time again," he growled.

"Seems so." Good thing I was too exhausted to stick my tongue out. I'd first met Gary when I'd discovered Jeff's body in the library in May. I had a paranoid feeling that he was going to blame me for this corpse.

"Why don't you tell me what happened here?" He pulled out a pen and notebook. "Don't leave out any details, even if you think they might be irrelevant."

He recorded my story impassively, and there really wasn't much to it. I was diving, I got caught in a rope tied to a rock, and there was a floating corpse secured to the rope's other end.

Gary never asked me why I was diving in the first place, and I wondered if he already knew about the diamond contest. He seemed to have an inside track on much of the town, possibly because of the off-hours "business ventures" he was rumored to have going with Kennie. I decided it didn't really matter. If he didn't know, I wasn't going to tell him.

He kept writing after I finished. When he finally snapped his notebook shut, he studied me for twenty long seconds, his expression unreadable. "You shouldn't dive alone."

"I know." I hated that he'd made a fair point. "Can I go?"

"You can, but don't stray too far from a phone. I might have more questions."

I nodded. The Mitsubishi owner offered me a ride home, and my still-shaky legs screamed at me to take it, but I wasn't going to relinquish the feeling of earth under my body, even if I had to crawl home. I thanked her but said I would walk. It was less than two miles, and even though I was wearing a wet suit and swim booties, it would be a welcome trek. The divers agreed to transport the rest of my equipment back to the Last Resort, including the BC once it was retrieved, and they sent me off with an apple and some string cheese.

Judging from the angle of the sun, it was pushing late afternoon. It truly was a beautiful day, and I had new appreciation for the warm air and the buzz of the leopard frogs in the sloughs. The apple was the best I'd ever eaten, and the tiny shock my muscles felt with each step on the pavement of County Road 82 was such ecstasy that I smiled at the passing cars.

I was alive, and I was on land.

I actually whistled until it became too painful for my vomit-seared throat. I'd managed to shove thoughts of my mother back into the mental detention room I reserved for my family, and I was back on an even keel. Thirty minutes later, turning down my half-mile driveway, I contemplated the wisdom of a nap. I was bone-tired, mentally and physically. I didn't want to tap out quite yet, though. I'd looked at the inside of my eyelids enough for one day.

After a shower, toothbrushing, and change of clothes, I found myself hiking back down to Sunny's little beach, where I'd taken off for my dive a lifetime ago. I stuffed the shorts, T-shirt, and flip-flops that I'd left at the shore into the bag I'd brought. Shading the sun from my eyes, I stared out at the to-do that was still happening on the lake. Two official-looking speedboats now circled my inner tube, but I didn't see an ambulance at the access, and there was only one police car visible. That surprised me. I'd learned in May that an ambulance was always called, even if the body was dead. There must be another tragedy tying up the county EMTs elsewhere.

And the body I'd found could certainly wait.

I glanced off to my right at the oak-shaded drive that led to Shangri-La, and without much thought, I started walking. I studied the bland rocks under my feet and considered what I would do when I reached the resort.

It didn't matter. I just wanted to keep walking.

I knew the owners, a retired married couple, Bing and Kellie Gibson. They'd bought the place three years earlier from the Blakers. The Blakers' main claim to fame, besides the resort, was that their son was Chuck Blaker, onetime host of the cheesy dating show *Love Language*. He used to visit them and eat at the local restaurants. That was juicy stuff in a small town like Battle Lake. We didn't see a lot of stars in the North Country.

The closest I'd come to someone famous in my proximity was Savannah, a classmate who'd appeared on *Puttin' on the Hits* the summer after our sophomore year. She mouthed and wiggled to "Shout" by Tears for Fears with the help of her cousin from Saint Paul. When she was in California filming her episode, she rode on the same elevator as Telly Savalas. She hadn't won, but that double dose of fame had been heady to all of us. We went around saying his trademark "Who loves ya, baby?" for most of our junior year of high school.

I thought of this as I came upon Shangri-La's main lodge and considered what I'd say to the Gibsons if they were around. They were a sweet couple and always went out of their way to talk to me whenever we crossed paths, but we'd never hung out socially. In fact, I'd never even been as far as Shangri-La and had only seen it from the lake.

Except for the beach, the whole place was heavily treed and private. The lakeside view hadn't done it justice. The main lodge was as big as a church. Its stained wood siding and cedar shakes blended beautifully with the oaks and birch shading the grounds. It matched the four servants' cottages that now served as cabins for guests who chose not to stay in the bed-and-breakfast that was the main lodge. The landscaping consisted of miniature lilacs, flowering chokecherry bushes, and shade-friendly perennials. An immaculate lawn ran the whole length of the beach. Judging from the piles of lake toys and fishing gear piled around, the place was booked.

I wondered what finding a dead body nearby was going to do to business.

I heard children giggling and spotted a group of four kids, all under ten or so, playing on the metal swing set on the far side of a cottage. I ducked around the front of the lodge so I wouldn't be seen. Then it occurred to me I'd probably be better off acting like I belonged here. I straightened out my hunch and told myself to walk with confidence. I rubbed my hands over my face and wiggled my nose, which was growing stiff with sunburn. I belonged here. The earth was my domain.

I strode around to the front of the lodge and past a group of three sitting on the front deck, sipping cold beers and speculating on what the boats were doing out front. I nodded at them like I was a guest, too, and strode inside.

If the lodge's exterior was spectacular, the interior was the Taj Mahal. The floors were a gleaming maple, rich and cherry-colored, the ceilings were fifteen feet high, and the decor was high-end rustic, mostly plaids and leather. A two-story fieldstone fireplace dominated the far wall. Altogether, it reminded me of a spacious English hunting lodge.

I remembered Shirly Tolverson saying the Addamses' bedroom had been upstairs, and that he'd caught Mrs. Krupps snooping there. That had started a suspicious chain of events: she lost a diamond necklace, Shirly and the other help were fired, and ultimately the Addamses sold the place.

I wanted to know what had gone down in that closet, but even more, I wanted to see what the bedroom of a fabulously wealthy couple looked like. The Gibsons had taken pains to keep the rest of the lodge authentic, and I was betting that the main bedroom was in spectacular shape. Look, I knew all the rooms upstairs were likely locked, but I was already here. Why not see for myself?

Voices echoed behind me as I tiptoed up the stairs. I needn't have bothered walking lightly. It was some guests, who ignored me as they walked past the dining hall and into another first-floor wing. I continued upward. The steps were hand carved out of expensive wood that wouldn't be caught dead creaking, so I again reminded myself I didn't need to sneak. If I ran into the Gibsons, I'd say I was there to tell them about the body I'd found. It seemed like a neighborly thing to do, and it was good cover.

It wasn't until I reached the top of the stairs that I really got a feel for the lodge's size. The steps wound up the middle of the building and divided the open-area landing of the second floor. If I went left or right off the stairs, I would walk in a square and be able to peer down into all the main rooms below. Off this square were eight doors, two on each side, and I guessed they all led to suites.

I walked around the first side but didn't try any of the doors because they all looked too mundane to be the bedroom of a man who'd name his summer home Shangri-La. Sure enough, when I reached the second side, I saw a hallway leading off, its entrance disguised by the angle. A string of triangular skylights illuminated the hallway, plump cherubs carved into the exquisite crown molding.

Bingo.

At the end of the hallway was a door straight out of Camelot. It had gilded leaves carved into its heavy wood, and the doorknob was a glittering crystal. It *had* to be the Addamses' bedroom.

I felt the knob with my hand. It was warm.

Then it started to turn.

Chapter 10

I leaped back, all excuses flying out of my head like popcorn. Why was I in the hallway of a lodge where I wasn't staying, about to go into a room where I didn't belong? Best to run. I turned away as the door opened, rushed my guilty hand through my hair, and hunched my shoulders to hide my face.

". . . the pile of rocks must be goddamn invisible if they're in that room, because I've—Mira?" The male voice behind me went from exasperated to dangerously annoyed.

I kept walking.

"Mira! What're you doing here?"

No point in pretending I was invisible. I swiveled to face Happy Hands, his sharp eyebrows drawn together in a V over his dark, angry eyes. "Hi, Jason." I would have been less surprised to see him at a spelling bee, but I tried to hide it.

He was decked out in zebra-striped Zubaz, a Coors Light tank top, and the same dock shoes he'd worn to accost me the night before. It seemed he hadn't traveled far since that encounter. He didn't appear much happier than he had when I'd last seen him, either.

I made a weak attempt at a joke. "No room at the parents', huh?"

He scowled but was shoved aside by a heavily jeweled hand. "Get out of my way, Jason! Gawd! You make a better window than a door."

The hand was followed by a bleached blonde with a heavy New York twang, probably in her early thirties but a heavy smoker, judging by her raspy voice and the premature crow's-feet around her eyes. She studied me. "You staying here?"

I smiled and held out my hand. "Nope, I live up the road. You a friend of Jason's?"

She rolled her eyes in an *unfortunately* kind of way and shook my hand. Her fingernails were long and red. I had a flash of insight. Had they left the scratches on Jason's back, either in ecstasy or pain?

"The big dope," she said, smiling at him. She rubbed his cheeks like he was a naughty child, even though he was a good seven inches taller and eighty pounds heavier. "I'm Samantha Krupps. Who're you?"

I jerked as if someone had stuck a live cattle prod in my back. *Krupps.* The last name of the woman who'd lost the original diamond necklace back in the twenties. "Mira James," I said, trying to keep my voice neutral. "You from around here?"

She smiled, her teeth a startling white against her poison-berry lipstick. "I'm from New York. Jason dragged me out here for a little vacation. Aren't we lucky that we found this place?"

Luck, indeed. I smelled something fishy, and it wasn't even me. "Where'd you two meet?"

"Oh, we—" Before Samantha could finish, Jason slammed the door shut behind him, locked it, grabbed her hand, and pulled her down the hall.

Before he disappeared around the corner, he turned to glare at me. "After you."

"I'm staying." I crossed my arms, feeling the same stubborn rush I did anytime someone told me what to do. "I want to talk to the Gibsons."

He released Samantha's hand, his grip leaving white marks on her skin, and strode toward me. He leaned down so we were nose to nose, his cologne eye-watering at this proximity. "The Gibsons went to town. You should go home. You look like shit."

The message was clear: he wasn't leaving until I was.

I could always come back when this ape wasn't guarding the room. It wouldn't cost me much to walk away right now, just a little pride. No way was he getting the last word in, though. "You know, Jason, you're kind of a dick."

I tried to sail past, my nose in the air, but he took my arm and twisted it behind me. The muscles wrenching burned like the snake-bites my friends and I used to give each other in grade school, but it didn't feel like Jason was going to stop before my skin slid off under his grip. I glared at him through the pain—he wasn't going to see that I was scared.

He opened his mouth to say something but thought better of it and instead shoved me toward the stairs. I was forced past Samantha, who was peeking over the stair rail.

"Nice meeting you," I said to her, wresting my arm away as Jason let up. I walked down the stairs, out the door, and up the road, acting like I was doing it of my own free will, like my arm didn't hurt at all.

I didn't start crying until I reached my driveway.

Luna ran up to greet me. I nuzzled into her neck, tears running into her fur. It was stupid. There was no point in crying. What I needed was time to think. Jason was looking for "rocks," and I didn't imagine he was after granite. He was in town with a Krupps and was clearly after far more than a $5,000 reward for a lost necklace.

I sat back on my heels, my tears stopping as I had a delicious realization. If I found the "rocks" first, Jason would most assuredly be pissed, maybe even feel betrayed and victimized.

I smiled.

The race was on.

Chapter 11

I hurried back to the double-wide, where I stacked sparkling water cans immediately inside the door so I'd be alerted if a stumbling corpse or Jason came after me. A quick look around assured me that everything was as I'd left it. The rust-colored sectional couch still dominated the front living area, the kitchen was still spotless, and there wasn't anyone in my bedroom, bathroom, or the laundry room.

The doors to the spare bedroom and office were closed, as they always were. I'd shoved most of Sunny's clutter into them when she left. I liked a lot of open space, and besides the bookshelves, television, and plants in the living room, there was nothing to dust. Tiger Pop and Luna watched as I finished my safety check before tearing open the fridge, ravenous. I grabbed a sleeve of honey wheat bagels and a tub of organic cream cheese. While a bagel toasted, I snatched the tomato off the windowsill where it'd been ripening and sliced it thin. When the bagel popped up, I smeared on a few tablespoons of cream cheese, stacked on as many fresh tomato slices as I could, and salted and peppered the whole pile.

The first bagel, I didn't taste. When I got halfway through the second one, I slowed down enough to enjoy it. Tiger Pop got bored watching me eat and found her favorite spot on the brown afghan draped over the couch, closing her eyes in ecstasy as she kneaded the yarn and soaked up a patch of sunlight. I'd named her after my second favorite candy (behind Nut Goodies, obvs), a sucker almost too sweet to eat and the same colors as my kitty—patches of white splashed through orange and red. Luna continued to watch me eat, ever hopeful. I tossed her the last bagel nub. She snapped it up midair.

Tummy full, I walked over to the fridge and pulled out a bottled water. The well water here was not drinkable, although a glassful would provide my mineral content for the day. The sinks were stained orange from it, and the tap always emitted a faint toilet smell. I carried the bottle of Aquafina into my bedroom, but at the sight of my bed, I realized I was too tired to drink or undress or even crawl under the blankets.

I tumbled forward and slept so hard that I dreamed I was sleeping.

The sun was cooling when I finally lurched out of bed, but I felt no more rested than before I'd lain down. A crisp shower and another change of clothes later, I found myself driving to the yellow-bricked Battle Lake Public Library. I'd decided I needed to go online to order a Taser, and I didn't have internet at Sunny's, and between the dead body and Jason's animosity, I was feeling a clear breach in personal security. I parked my car in the empty library lot but decided to run to the Fortune Café for some green tea before going in. I hoped they'd still be open.

The streets were busy for a Sunday night, several cars driving past, people out walking—including a couple coming toward me. We were ten feet apart before I realized it was the Gibsons, my neighbors and the owners of Shangri-La. I considered turning around and walking the other way, but they'd seen me.

Bing was a short man, maybe five foot five, and his head was entirely hairless except for bushy white eyebrows, which perched like an umlaut on his face. He'd been a pilot in a previous life and carried himself with quiet confidence. Kellie was the tall one, pushing five eight, and she always wore her long gray hair in a french twist. She and Bing had met after he'd broken his leg in a skiing accident and been referred to the clinic where she was a physical therapist. Now they both were living out their dream of owning a resort.

"Mira! How're you doing?" Kellie smiled warmly at me. Bing did the same.

I suddenly felt personally responsible for the existence of a dead body in front of their resort and ducked my head. "I'm good." I wondered if they knew. According to Jason, they hadn't been at Shangri-La when I'd been attacked by the corpse. I sure didn't want to be the one to tell them. "How's business?"

They glanced at each other and chuckled. "Good enough to raise the dead," Kellie said, stifling a guffaw.

I recoiled. If they knew about the body, that was one heck of a tacky thing to say. "I don't know what's funny."

Bing leaned forward and put his hand on my arm. "Didn't you hear? A diver came across what she thought was a drowning victim on Whiskey Lake early this afternoon. Right out front of our beach, matter of fact. Turns out it was just a stuffed wet suit tied to a rock and made to look like a dead body."

My eyes grew big, and I had a genuine coughing fit. I'd almost gotten myself drowned next to a *fake corpse*?? Geez Louise. At least the Gibsons didn't know I was the diver. I fought the urge to defend the lack of visibility underwater.

"That's wild," I said, playing it cool. "Why would anyone dump a fake dead body in Whiskey Lake?"

Kellie screwed up her face, her blue eyes twinkling. "Probably some attention-getting prank related to the *Pioneer Press* contest."

Boy, these two had a knack for making me feel dumb. "You guys know about the necklace?"

"It was actually my idea," Kellie said, managing to sound modest. "I have a friend at the newspaper, and she passed the idea on to the woman who wrote the article. It's fun, don't you think?"

"Yeah, buckets of fun." *Wish you'd told us over at the* Battle Lake Recall.

"You dive, don't you, Mira? You should get a wet suit and join the fun!" She gave me an end-of-conversation smile and started walking away, Bing at her side.

"We'll see you around," he called over his shoulder. "In fact, you should drop by the resort tomorrow night. The Romanov Traveling Theater troupe has agreed to give an outdoor performance, weather permitting. It's going to be a jungle magic show with jugglers and mimes and bongo players!"

That's what the doctor ordered—a night with a mime at a resort where I'd biffed across a fake dead body and where my Zubaz-pantsed nemesis was staying. If only we could include axe-wielding clowns and pop-up mammograms, it'd be like Christmas in June.

It was enough to make a gal start smoking again.

Chapter 12

I was relieved to find the Fortune Café open late. The coffee shop was owned by Sid and Nancy, two local lesbians, who—for some inexplicable reason—the town referred to as "the women who played cards." It was a Lutheran euphemism that I did not get, and if they were handing out nicknames based on who we slept with, I didn't want to know what they were calling me.

Sid wore her hair short and spiky and preferred flannel, even in the summer, and Nancy had flowing, Crystal Gayle brown hair that she pulled back with butterfly pins. Nancy's life motto was "Shit or get off the pot," and she had a plaque proclaiming as much inside the café's bathroom. If people wanted to believe it referred to their restroom activities, that was their business.

The whole place smelled like cinnamon and fresh bread, and the Fortune served the best decaf mochas and ginger scones this side of the Cities. The main room was stocked with their personal book collection, mostly mysteries and true crime novels, and comfy furniture. I spent many a free hour there reading, sipping tea or coffee, and playing Scrabble with Sid when business was slow. Nancy didn't like board games.

During one of our word fests, I'd asked Sid why she and Nancy had landed in Battle Lake. Like many a small town, this one had its share of small minds who would not line up to give two proud women who happened to be gay the key to the city. Shoot, I still encountered people here who looked down their nose at me because I hadn't been born in Battle Lake.

Sid spelled out "QUINCE" and took a sip of her coffee. "There's small minds everywhere, Mira. You can't make choices based on fear."

"I don't know." I counted the points she'd just earned. "I make some of my best choices based on fear."

Sid smiled. "Nancy and I both grew up in towns the size of Battle Lake. We like the pace and the familiarity. Plus, this is the only coffee shop we found that we could afford."

"Ha! So it *was* money that brought you here."

"That, and the gorgeous lake and smiling faces of the locals and Pastor Winter's great sermons. Just give it some time, Mira, and you'll be stuck here, too. In a good way. This town has a lot to offer."

I laid the *D, I,* and *S* tiles in front of the word "BELIEF" that she'd played four turns ago. Fifteen points, doubled because the *D* fell on a pink. I loved it when things worked out like that. As I added my score, a piece of trivia floated up. "Did you know that Alfred M. Butts invented Scrabble?"

"Yeah, and I. M. Sapphic is going to win it," she said. "Pay attention!"

I smiled at the memory as I approached Sid, who was working behind the counter. The place was jumping, and I had to wait to order. By the time I reached the front, the smell of fresh-roasted coffee beans pushed the thought of ordering green tea out my ear.

"Mira! Is it too late in the night for your decaf mocha?" she asked.

"Only if you didn't just find a fake corpse in Whiskey Lake."

"That was you!" she crowed. She turned toward the kitchen. "Nance! That dead body in Whiskey Lake, that wasn't really dead or a body? Guess who found it!"

Nancy appeared from behind the swinging door, wiping her flour-covered hands on an apron that read "One Recruit Short of a Toaster Oven." She grinned broadly when she saw me, her bright smile gentling her rough features. "My money is on our resident body-finder, Ms. James herself."

"Bingo." I fished in the pockets of my cutoffs for money. "Since you guys already heard about Mr. Boddy, I suppose you've also heard about the diamond necklace and the *Pioneer Press* contest?"

"Old news, sweets," Nancy said, lacing her arm around Sid's waist. "Tell Ron to get his hands out of his wife's pants and onto a keyboard, preferably with a washing in between. Most of the town knows about the contest."

"Why am I always the last one to hear?" I asked.

"You're an outsider, hon." Sid kissed the top of Nancy's head. "It takes a while for this town to accept you."

"Pshaw," I said, my chest warming nicely. Seeing good people in love was one of my favorite things. "Give me some coffee. I'm off to order a Taser followed possibly by a couple drinks at Clyde's to discover what *else* everyone knows that I don't."

Sid operated the gurgling barista machine and added extra chocolate and whipped cream to my drink. She slid it across the counter. "Two-fifty. Anything else?"

"Call me if you hear something that sounds like news, 'kay? I'm supposed to be a reporter."

She nodded solemnly. "You got it."

"Thanks."

I sipped gingerly at the creamy, hot coffee, which felt like manna on my raw throat, and headed out the door in search of weaponry and answers.

Chapter 13

On Sunday nights, the weekend tourists normally packed up and returned to the Cities, leaving Battle Lake relatively quiet. This evening was different, however, the crowds growing since I'd gone into the Fortune. The plastic chairs outside Granny's Pantry were full of sticky kids nursing triple-decker waffle cones and playing tag around their parents' legs, several couples strolled hand in hand, and a group of folks peered inside the Village Apothecary.

The diamond contest was bringing people in.

When I reached the library, I fished in my pockets for the keys. Lartel McManus, the former head librarian, had always kept a key under the fake rock out front. He'd disappeared in May, shortly after Jeff was killed. While he'd put his house up for sale, it was still on the market, so there was always a possibility that he might return. When I landed his job until the city could hire a properly qualified librarian, I'd convinced the town to change the locks.

I was now the only one who held the keys, and I kept the place clean. That's why Kennie's Minnesota Nice brochure with a paper pocket full of business cards stuck to the door immediately caught my attention. I ripped it off to move it inside to the foyer.

The smell of old paper and slick magazines was still the first thing to greet me, but since I'd started steering the ship, there was a whiff of sandalwood incense as well. There were also far more plants, mostly ferns and succulents, which were my favorites. I had them lusciously packed in the windows. If the sun fell just right, the kids' area under the south window lit up like a jungle.

I marched straight to the front desk computer, booted it up, and started clacking away at an article on the diamond necklace. I added some angles from my interview with Shirly without revealing his reluctance to confirm the diamond was real or his suspicion there'd been something fishy going on at Shangri-La that summer. Those were things I wanted to look into for myself first. I proofread the article until I was satisfied it was error-free and not too obviously plagiarized from the *Pioneer Press* and attached it to an email to Ron.

After I clicked "Send," I ran a search on "Taser." I didn't really know what they were beyond a quick and legal way to defend myself. My research informed me that Tasers shot little electric bullets, nonlethal and nonpenetrating, which resulted in "electro-muscular disruption." I gathered this was cop-speak for "You'll be so juiced that it'll be half an hour before you can slap a mosquito off your own ass."

Unfortunately, the Tasers were out of my price range, so I opted for a fifty-five-dollar Z-Force stun gun, which promised to deliver 300,000 volts to any creep who got within arm's reach. It resembled a mean black flashlight with two metal prongs at one end. I knew I'd have a hard time not immediately testing it out, but I had a hunch fate would provide me with that opportunity soon, and I was old enough to know you should always listen to your hunches. I paid twenty-five extra bucks for same-day shipping, shut down the computer, and took off for Bonnie & Clyde's.

Once on the road, I cranked open my window to let the frog songs and sweet green breeze wash in. Minnesota was an incredible place to live, but we natives learned at a young age that for this privilege we must pay a tithe, usually in blood. We're first indoctrinated while we're still in diapers. A summer day spent in the shallow, still part of the lake would result in chocolate chip–shaped leeches nesting between our peas-in-a-pod toes. That would lead to the wood tick that attached itself to the front of our earlobe when we were five. Thinking it was the closest we'd come to an earring for many years, we'd manage to hide it from our mom until it's a corpulent gray blob, its legs ridiculously small on its blood-stressed body. Oh, let's not forget the omnipresent mosquitoes.

And that was only summer.

When winter arrived, it brought winds so fierce that school was sometimes canceled simply because it was too cold to step outside.

Minnesota was not a place for the faint of heart, and we wouldn't have it any other way.

It was a quiet acceptance of these dynamics that made every Minnesotan welcome at Bonnie & Clyde's, one of two bars and four total businesses in Clitherall, if you counted the post office. It was a seven-minute ride from Battle Lake to Clitherall, and I drove sixty the whole way, slowing only to pass Delbert Larsen. He was driving his riding lawn mower on the shoulder of Highway 210, and I didn't want to roar past him. Delbert had gotten his license revoked after his fifth DWI, but he wasn't letting that put a dent in his good times. I waved as I passed.

He made the classic "old man shaking his fist" gesture back at me. Crabby bastard.

When I entered Clyde's, the cigarette smoke and pounding notes of Kid Rock raced for purchase in all my orifices, big and small. The smoke won, but the music got my hips moving. The bar was a visual disharmony of wood and lights, with holes in the floor that allowed customers to watch Ruby change kegs below, and bathroom doors that didn't lock. The chairs were plastic, public school–style, and the tables were mismatched, some of them handmade and some of them folding card tables. This comfortable rot was contrasted with a sparkly, modern jukebox, pristine pool tables, and a buttery, elegant main bar. I tried to look cool as I strode forward, planning to stare down anyone who glanced at the jangling of the door opening, but I needn't have bothered. The place was empty except for Ruby, who was the bartender and owner, Jed, and Johnny.

What.

My heart pumped some extra blood to my cooter. What had I done to deserve two Johnny Leeson sightings in one day? I took a hard left to the bar instead of saying hi, though Jed and Johnny had both tossed me smiles. I envied women who could flirt, those easygoing, hair-flipping, throaty-laughed sirens. I just wasn't comfortable putting myself out there. When confronted by an attractive man, the best I could rustle up was an attention-deflecting sarcastic remark and a stiff smile. If my dating track record was any indication, that was exactly the mating dance of the emotionally unavailable male of the species for whom foreplay was a card game.

"Hi, Ruby. Got any specials tonight?"

Ruby was in her early seventies and had owned Bonnie & Clyde's for decades. Her husband built the place, and she'd kept it running after he died. She ignored me like she ignored all her customers, continuing to shove beer glasses upside down on the rotating scrubbers in the first of three sinks she used to wash barware. The second sink rinsed the soap off, and the third sanitized with some blue cleansing agent. Or at least it would have, if the toxicity of Clitherall's water didn't create a chemical reaction that made the blue tablet black and the water smell like broccoli.

Sunny had told me that a couple years earlier, a sales rep had come to Clyde's trying to sell a gross of cocktail napkins that patrons could splash a drop or two of their drink onto to see if it had been spiked. Ruby had laughed out loud. She knew the nitrates in the water neutralized everything but alcohol, for good or ill. It was part of the place's charm, and before you worry too much, you should know that Clitherall was the home of the oldest married couple in the five-state area. The water couldn't be all bad.

Ruby swiped her wet hands on her jeans, tipped up one of the still-dripping beer glasses, and poured me a Lite draft. I thanked her, slid four singles onto the low spot of the bar, and watched her hands carefully. She had a way of taking my money and assuming her tip without me ever seeing it. The game was worth the gratuity.

I was considering how long I should let the beer sit in my glass before the alcohol killed the nitrates, or vice versa, when there was a tap on my shoulder.

"Mira, hey, cool. Why don't you come hang out with me and Johnny?"

I turned to Jed, thinking I'd like to hang *off* Johnny. I had a momentary flash of worry that Johnny might be a pothead if he hung around with Jed, but then I remembered *I* hung out with Jed, too. I think the three of us didn't bump into one another more often because Johnny was so busy. On top of his job at the nursery, he played in a local band and gave piano lessons.

He was a Battle Lake native who'd left for the University of Wisconsin to study botany five years earlier. I didn't know if he had finished his degree or not, but I *did* know he'd returned to his hometown last summer under less-than-happy circumstances. My local friend Gina said he got kicked out of the university for knifing a guy or stealing rare plants from the college greenhouse, she wasn't sure which.

I refused to believe either.

I leaned over to check him out, admiring his strong hands and muscular arms as he tipped his head back to finish his beer. He was bright and healthy and open. *Clearly* not my type. With the exception of my short tryst with Jeff, I went for the dark brooders, the guys who disguised their dum-dum behind a wall of quiet. I'd even dated one hot slacker because he liked dark chocolate. I'd wanted to believe that was proof of his intelligence, but I had to release that illusion after he let me read his poetry. It all rhymed, every poem about the band Van Halen. My favorite was titled "David Lee Roth, Thou Art the Flame to My Moth."

No, Johnny would definitely stand out among the short lineup of my past loves. *Dang his earthy appeal.* I wanted to get down and dirty with him, literally. But even if he and I were the same species, which we clearly weren't, he was in a relationship, and I respected that. Come to think of it, that meant he was entirely off limits, which meant I could hang out with him without devolving into a puddle of dork.

Right?

"Sure thing," I told Jed, sliding off the stool.

"Hey, Jay, Mira wants to hang with us!" Jed said, leading me over.

I held out my hand and smiled into Johnny's eyes. "Twice in one day. It must be fate."

At least, that's what I swear to God I meant to say. Johnny was taken, I was cool, we could be friends. So why did my mouth instead blurt out, "Twice in one day. This lust can't wait."

Nooooooooooooo.

I melted into a flaming pile of shame. I honestly shouldn't be let out of the house. Johnny held on to my hand and leaned his ear close to my mouth. "What?"

Had the blaring jukebox covered my words? I breathed the clean spice of his thick, sun-kissed hair, and lightning bolts shot out of my crotch. If smoke started rising from my nether region, I'd have to pack up and move to Australia—sorry, Battle Lake.

"I just said it's nice to see you again," I said loudly, thinking quickly. "You know, here at Bonnie & Clyde's, where before it was at the Last Resort." That put me one sentence past cool.

He nodded. "Yeah. Say, I enjoyed that article on Jeff Wilson."

Sweet Mary. He gardened, smoldered, *and* read. I was way out of my league.

"And I plant your stuff in my garden," I said, following this ridiculous observation with a twinkly guffaw that crescendoed into a snort. Even Jed was starting to notice my lack of cool. I poured beer into my mouth before I said something else stupid.

For his part, Johnny smiled brilliantly and returned to the pool game. When he was out of earshot, I turned to Jed. "Why am I such a dork?"

"Dorks rule, man," he said, nodding happily. "Wanna get high?"

"No thanks." I patted his shoulder. "How're you doing tonight?"

His sweet eyes grew wide, his curls bobbing as he shook his head. He was a cross between Shaggy from *Scooby-Doo* and a Muppet. "Except for a little too much time with the Man, I'm good," he said. "Shit, I thought they were coming for me."

I pulled my attention from Johnny, who was leaning deliciously across the pool table as he lined up the purple four ball with the corner pocket. "The cops?"

"The *cop*," Jed corrected, tugging nervously at his Pink Floyd T-shirt. "Gary Wohnt stopped by the Last Resort, dude, his cherries spinning. I had my stash flushed before he got to the main office. Good thing I only had a dime bag."

My forehead furrowed. "He came to bust you?"

"Naw, and that's the kicker!" Jed slapped his knee. "He wanted a list of who we rented dive gear to. That fake body they found in Whiskey? It was wearing a Last Resort wet suit. We stamp the name on every one of 'em. Right on the butt."

I wanted to laugh along with Jed, but every time someone talked about that planted body, it tossed me into the deep end of the shame pool. It felt like a big joke at my expense. One that'd almost killed me. "So who *did* you provide gear for?"

"Aw, some tourists staying at Shangri-La, a couple staying at the Last Resort, and you."

"No one you recognized?"

"No one except Jason Blunt. You know him, don't you? I think he used to date Sunny back in the day. Boy, could that dude put away a bong. He had a mean streak like a mule if you crossed him, though."

My heart made its way out of my chest and lumped in my throat. "Jason rented a dive suit from you?"

"Three dive suits, three BCs, three of everything. The day before you got yours. Why? You think he planted the body?"

A heaviness pushed down onto my shoulders. I'd had enough Jason for one day. Scratch that. For a lifetime. "That's totally possible." The question was why. "Hey, I think I'm tapped. I'm gonna head out."

I brought my unfinished beer to the counter and saw that my four dollars had disappeared even though Ruby had been at the far end of the bar the entire time I'd been talking to Johnny and Jed. I waved a quick goodbye to both and imagined for a moment that Johnny's eyes lingered on my mouth as he smiled at me.

No, must have been the lighting. Anyhow, I was too concerned about Jason's current nastiness to have more than a parting lustful thought about Johnny Leeson. It was a vivid one, though.

Which was why I deserved every bad thing that happened to me after that.

Chapter 14

I slept fitfully that night and woke at least four times, wishing I had my stun gun under my pillow. On the fifth wake-up, I seriously considered moving myself to a corner of the spare room under all Sunny's stored junk. An intruder wouldn't look for me there, and I could catch some z's. I quickly discarded that idea, though, refusing to be scared in my own bed in my own home.

Instead, I gave up wrestling with the sandman and took my knotty head outside. The stars were fading, and the air was hot on cool, the left-overs of a ninety-degree day losing out to the quiet morning chill. The wild animals didn't know whether to make night or morning sounds, and my presence threw another wrench into their song. I sat on the front deck, closing my eyes so I could better hear the rustlings in the woods and smell the mystery of Whiskey Lake. I could feel the reper-cussions of yesterday's dive in my sunburned nose and the tightness of my shoulders as I stretched.

I soon realized I wasn't comfortable sitting, either. Tired as I was, I still had too much nervous energy. I got off my butt, the shorts I'd thrown on wet from the dew, and walked past the barn down to my vegetable garden. I'd tilled this area in early May, and though I still had to fight the pigweed and thistle for ownership, it was turning out to be a good location with a full day of sun.

The marigolds I'd planted were the tallest growths. I could smell their bitterness even with their orange and yellow heads closed to the dropping moon. My mother had taught me to plant a thick square of marigolds and lavender first thing around a vegetable garden. With their natural insecticide properties, they were soldiers guarding my zucchini, carrot, bean, pea, and corn sprouts.

I'd learned everything I knew about gardening from her. Every summer, she tilled up a huge section of open land between the hobby farm outbuildings and planted every vegetable that might grow in west central Minnesota—and some, like garlic and sweet potatoes, that might not. She was a gifted and optimistic gardener, and although I'd hated planting and weeding when I was younger, I'd loved to watch her face when she worked. All the lines left her forehead and around her mouth, and although she never looked *happy*, she seemed peaceful, like she was in the right place at the right time.

She only looked like that when she was in her garden.

She'd be pleased to know I'd planted dill alongside my veggies. I'd chosen the herb for two reasons. First, it would repel aphids as well as the spider mites attracted by my marigolds, on top of drawing the tomato worms away from my heirloom Red Brandywines. Second, although I had a fairly green thumb, I'd never been able to grow cucumbers to save my soul. Try as I might in many different soils with many different varieties, from Tendergreen Burpless to white spine, I couldn't get the seedlings to thrive past germination. I planned for the dill to serve as an enticement, like, "If you grow, I'll let you be a pickle."

Pickling was the Valhalla of the vegetable world.

I stepped through the opening I'd left in my bug-fighting border and mucked over to the far side of my plot. The black dirt was still warm from yesterday's sun. My toes squished through the top layer of dewmud and into the looser earth below. I knelt at the head of the carrot row, one knee on each side. The shaggy sprouts were thick; I didn't have enough patience to plant the microscopic seeds carefully or the heart to thin them after they sprouted, so I treated carrots as an ornamental crop.

The moon was full enough for me to distinguish carrot from weed, and I quickly got my method down, popping the thistle and leafy spurge easily from the moist ground. As I worked, my knees sank into the dirt and my mind focused. Jason was back in town, and he'd brought with him Samantha Krupps, who was likely related to the woman who'd "lost" the necklace in Whiskey Lake decades ago.

Shirly had suggested there was more to the original Krupps story than simply a lost necklace, and overhearing Jason in the owner's suite at Shangri-La had confirmed his belief that Mrs. Krupps had hidden something in that room. Maybe it was the diamond necklace along with the rest of the jewels that had gone missing that summer long ago.

I was sure if I could sneak into the bedroom, I could find the jewels. This feeling was probably tied to my childhood as a stasher. Back then, hiding valuables had given me a feeling of control over my life. I hid flattened dollar bills in the cracks of a window sash, sea glass in the knothole in my closet, my diary under my bedsprings.

My favorite hoard had been a cache of glittering rhinestones that I'd started collecting at garage sales when I was six. I'd save up my allowance and scour the old jewelry piled on the front card table of every sale. After many years, I'd acquired quite a collection, one still hidden in the floorboards of my old bedroom. It gave me something secret to think about, something that made me happy.

Had Mrs. Krupps had the same urge all those years ago?

I just didn't understand how the *Pioneer Press* piece tied into Jason and Samantha's appearance. Was it coincidence that the newspaper article ran around the same time they'd arrived, or was there a bigger plan unfolding here, one beyond my vision?

And what would Jason and Samantha gain by planting a fake dead body in Whiskey Lake? If they hoped to scare off people looking for the contest's necklace, their time would have been better spent searching for the real jewel, since the comment I'd overheard Jason making suggested he believed it existed. This made me wonder whether the Gibsons were in on it. Kellie said she'd tipped the newspaper to the whole necklace story. Had they told Jason, too, and if so, why?

Clearly, I'd need to do some investigative reporting at the Romanov show at Shangri-La, despite my misgivings about crowds and theater types. Didn't hurt that it'd give me a cover to sneak into the Addamses' bedroom.

I'd reached the peas. Their vines were so extensive I had to flip them side to side like long green hair over dirt shoulders to reach the weeds beneath. I would have kept weeding, ignoring the tangerine and cream of the rising sun, if the melancholy cry of a loon on the lake hadn't pulled me out of my reverie. I sat back on my heels and searched for the bird, but the shadows played tricks on my eyes. I brushed off my knees and went inside.

After a long, refreshing shower, I slapped on some ChapStick, made a yogurt and frozen banana smoothie, and headed to town to grab a copy of the *Recall* and open up the library.

My article was on the front page. I had titled it "Find One Diamond Today" because it had an internal rhyme, and I hoped the "Today" made it sound fresh:

> A day in paradise could end up being a week in Shangri-La for the lucky person who finds the fake diamond planted in Otter Tail County's Whiskey Lake. The Saint Paul *Pioneer Press*, tipped off to a local legend, has placed a weighted box containing a paste diamond into the lake, which lies south of Battle Lake on Highway 78. People may begin diving for it today, and whoever is fortunate enough to discover it will receive $5,000 and a paid week at Shangri-La, the historic luxury resort owned by Kellie and Bing Gibson.
>
> "[The contest] was actually my idea," Kellie Gibson said modestly. "I have a friend at the newspaper, and

she passed the idea on to the woman who wrote the article."

Gibson's idea holds deep appeal. According to Shirly Tolverson, local amateur historian, Randolph Addams built Shangri-La in the 1920s to be his summer home. When it was complete, it consisted of a beautiful main lodge (what Addams called his "little cabin") and four cottages for the staff, all nestled on the six-acre peninsula jutting into Whiskey Lake. During the summer of 1929, a Mrs. Krupps from New York was a guest at the Addamses' lodge. While swimming, she lost the necklace she was wearing, an enormous dew-drop diamond on a gold chain.

According to Tolverson, who was working at Shangri-La the summer the necklace disappeared, "I saw her stroll into the water with a diamond the size of a car-amel around her neck. I saw her walk out of the water without it." The guests and staff, including Tolverson, searched frantically for the missing necklace. The di-amond was never found. Local legend has it that it is still in the lake, waiting to be discovered.

The *Pioneer Press* contest, designed to bring atten-tion to Battle Lake's beautiful topography and tourist appeal, was based on locating a fake diamond, but who knows? Maybe some lucky diver will find the real thing.

I folded the paper, not entirely happy with my article. There was too much I didn't know. All I could do now, though, was wait for the morning crowd to arrive for Monday Madness. That's what I called the children's reading hour I hosted every Monday morning at ten. I thought it was a funny name, what with all the kids screaming and picking and scratching at themselves as I tried to imitate perkiness while reading to them. It was my one shot to infiltrate their young minds, though, and I enjoyed it. The kids liked books for all the right reasons, and they were mostly cute, even if they had the attention span of hair on fire.

The only thing I dreaded about Monday Madness was dealing with Leylanda Bertram, who brought her seven-year-old daughter, Peyton, to every reading. Peyton was aggrieved by the constant demands of the nonprincess existence she was forced to live.

It was pretty cute on a little girl.

Unfortunately, her mother had the same attitude. On top of walking around with her nose in the air, she regularly complained that I only chose books about independent girls (she was right) who usually defied society's rules (right again) and that I didn't give enough time to the "classics" like "Snow White" and "Cinderella."

This morning, she wore an immaculate and stiff dress suit, clutching her purse as if she carried her spare heart in it, Peyton dragging behind.

"Peyton, we will stay for one-half of an hour if Ms. James is reading good stories," she was saying. "If not, I will read you one story of your choosing no longer than ten minutes in length, and then we will go to Meadow Farm Foods to buy some free-range chicken and delicious whole grains."

Peyton rolled her eyes at me. I nodded and rolled mine back. Leylanda was the worst kind of creature—a conservative disguised as a granola. She even wore Birkenstocks with her pressed Tommy Hilfiger jeans and polos.

"Hey, Leylanda," I said. "Today I'm going to read a book about a little boy and a princess who fall in love and get married."

Leylanda eyed me suspiciously from behind her trendy, dark-rimmed glasses. "What's it called?"

"*Prince Cinders*. I think Peyton'll like it."

I grabbed Peyton's hand and pulled her to the front of the yammering crowd of kids before her mom could object. The story was one of my favorites, a gender-flipped Cinderella story. The kids loved it.

I read a couple more keepers and then returned the squirmers to their parents, who were scattered around the library reading paperbacks and magazines. Back at the front desk, I sorted through the books that'd been returned. A lot of people were streaming through already, which was unusual for ten thirty on a Monday. I counted heads and wondered how many were here because of the diamond necklace contest. That was when Kennie walked in.

My heart dropped.

"Hey, sugar doll. What's up?" she asked.

Today, she was dressed like the sun. She wore acid-yellow jelly shoes, yellow-striped pedal pushers, a plastic yellow belt with a brass buckle, and a yellow tank top made of some water-, flame-, and possibly bulletproof material. Her canary-colored sunglasses were perched on her head, but they weren't bright enough to distract from her lemon-shaded earrings that looked straight out of a blind man's tackle box. All this splendor was arranged around a camel toe the size of Egypt.

And just like that, I had my idea.

"Not much, Kennie. Say, you still doing that Minnesota Nice business?"

She rushed over to me like I was the last krumkake at a church bake sale. "Why, yes I am! In fact, I'm here to drop off some more flyers. Do you know someone who needs the hard truth?"

I smiled so broadly that the corners of my mouth got my eyes wet. "Sort of. It's more about justice than honesty. You free tonight?"

"Hmm. Let me see." From her yellow plastic tote bag, she pulled out a cardboard folder with a picture of two adorable kittens on the front, one sleeping on a branch and the other one clinging to the wood by one slipping claw. Underneath the photo were the words ONLY THE STRONG SURVIVE.

"You're in luck. Tonight is open. What'd you have in mind?" She leaned forward on the counter, squishing her boobs together over a Grand Canyon of cleavage. I caught a solid waft of her signature scent: yeasty gardenias.

"There's this guy in town, Jason Blunt. He used to be my boyfriend, long ago, and I was really into him. In fact, I think he might have been The One."

Kennie hid her doubt with the professionalism of a free-clinic gynecologist. "Go on."

"Well, I caught him cheating on me. Like I said, he's back in town, and I—"

"And you want me to make his life hell tonight?"

"Yep, uh-huh. I know it's a little bit outside the purview of your Minnesota Nice business, but I thought you could maybe turn on the Kennie charm and show him a good time."

"And then dump him cold, like he dumped you?"

"Sure." I was actually thinking a night fending off Kennie's advances would be its own dose of strap oil, but whatever she needed to play this scene was fine by me. She'd buy me some time to snoop, and he'd have an evening of hell.

But then I realized I couldn't send her to the wolves, no matter how much I wanted Jason to suffer. "I'm sorry, Kennie. That was a lie. The truth is Jason's a creeper. He attacked me about ten years ago, and now he's back in town."

It had been surprisingly hard to say that out loud.

Her eyes glittered. "He hurt you bad?"

"Not really," I said. "Honestly, it might not have even been an attack. It only lasted a couple minutes."

"Don't."

"What?"

"Don't do that." She looked artificial, top to toe, but her words came out as real as could be. "Don't cut down what you felt. If you think you were attacked, you were attacked."

I wasn't prepared for the wave of emotion. She watched me, her eyes calculating, then said, "I'd be happy to make him suffer."

My heart leaped, then dropped back to earth. "He might be dangerous."

"I'll keep it public."

This might work. "He's got a girlfriend with him, so you'd need to sidestep her."

Kennie nodded, making her gargantuan earrings jingle. "Where can I find him?"

So this was what it felt like to be completely satisfied. *Meow.*

"He's staying at Shangri-La, and I'm pretty sure he'll be at the Romanov Traveling Theater performance tonight."

"He won't know what hit him."

I was banking on it.

Chapter 15

On the way home from my long day at the library, I stopped at the Turtle Stew for some broasted chicken and jo-jos to go. The Stew was my favorite restaurant in town. They made a mean Tater Tot hotdish and had authentic Naugahyde booths. It was a great place to people-watch, too.

When I was ordering my food, it occurred to me that I missed my friend Gina, so I ordered double of everything and took it to her house. I'd met her through Sunny more than a decade earlier, at the annual Chief Wenonga Days street dance. Gina and Sunny had graduated high school together and both gone on to work at the Otter Tail County nursing home, one of the few local jobs besides waitressing that a person without a college education could get by on. The two of them were tied together due to a shared history, but I loved Gina for her uncomplicated, honest company.

She was in her late twenties, built like a blonde fire hydrant, and married to her grade-school sweetheart, Leif Hokum. When I'd met him, I'd joked that it would be helpful if all potential mates came clearly labeled like that. When I realized the last name of my job-free boyfriend at the time was Kidd, I wondered if maybe they *did* all come plainly labeled—God's apology for poor clitoris placement—and we just had to look to see it.

When I reached Gina's one-story house on the north side of town, she answered the door wearing duck-print scrubs. She worked four twelve-hour shifts a week, with alternating weekends. It left her so constantly tired that I hardly ever saw her.

She seemed exhausted but grateful at the sight of me.

"Hey, chickie," I said, hugging her. "Where's Leif?"

She grabbed the carton of broasted chicken from my hand and made her way to the sofa. "Probably fishing."

Gina's husband was the typical Otter Tail County man. He was tall, dirty blond, and sporting a burgeoning beer belly. When he wasn't hunting with his gun, bow, or crossbow, he was ice fishing, river fishing, lake fishing, or spear fishing. All this self-reliance might be awesome if a person found himself suddenly transplanted to *Little House on the Prairie*–era Minnesota, but it took a bite out of modern-day relationships.

"Don't you get sick of him being gone all the time?"

She shrugged and leaned back on the couch, rearranging the walleye-shaped pillows so she could get comfortable. "He's here when I need him. Besides, we just had a great talk the other night. We both agreed we need to communicate better and have more fun together."

Sounded good to me. "What's the plan to pull that off?"

"Drink more." She ripped a chunk of breast meat off the bone. "Dang, this was the longest day ever! We admitted four new residents and had a surprise visit from the state. I feel like all I do is go to work, come home, eat, watch some TV, and go to bed. And they pay me just enough to get up the next day and do it all over again. You gonna eat all those jo-jos?"

I passed her the greasy wax bag and took a pull on my Dr Pepper. "You do look tired."

"You think? That's why nobody around here is winning any think-offs. Too much work. By the end of the day, all we want to do is watch *Full House* and go to bed." Her eyes focused on me, and her voice changed from complaining to curious. "Say, I hear Jason Blunt is staying at Shangri-La."

I knew Gina would get to the heart of my problems pretty quick. She always did. "Who told?"

"Linda Gundersen, who's friends with Jason's mom. She stopped by the nursing home to visit her aunt. She said Jason's mom was in a snit because Jason's girlfriend said she was 'too good' to stay at their single-wide."

I snorted. "Shoot. Trailers were made for people like those two. Yeah, he's in town. He visited my bedroom the night before last. Thought I was Sunny."

Gina nodded knowingly. "Horn call."

"Yup. And it was a wrong number." I chewed another jo-jo. "I can't imagine how tight he is with this 'girlfriend' he brought to town if he's already sleeping around."

"That don't mean anything with Blunt. He could be married to Tyra Banks and he'd still stick his pork and beans in a tree if he thought he wouldn't get caught."

I had to agree. I filled her in on my interview with Shirly and the questions it raised as well as my disastrous diving expedition. I didn't mention overhearing Jason talk about the jewels he was after because I didn't want any rumors starting, but I did tell her I was visiting Shangri-La tonight.

This reminded me of Kennie in her full splendor, making a little love magic for Jason.

"What're you smiling at?" Gina grinned back, her green eyes crinkling at the corners. She had a circle of grease around her mouth that she swiped at with a napkin.

"Nothing," I said. "I gotta go, anyhow. The Shangri-La show starts soon." I waved my hand at the chicken. "Give Leif the rest of the food. It'd be good for him to see that you can *buy* meat, too."

I was halfway to my car before I had a thought. I returned to the house and poked my head in to see Gina gnawing at a leg bone. "Hey, queen of the jungle, I don't suppose that Jason's mom's friend Linda Gundersen mentioned where in New York Jason's haughty girlfriend is from?"

"I don't know where she was born, but she lives in Niagara County now. I remember because I didn't know it was a county. Think Niagara Falls is in Niagara County?"

"It'd make sense. Mind if I use your computer for a minute?"

"Nope." She wiped her hands on a napkin. "Just ignore the screen saver."

Said screen saver was a picture of two deer watching a man and a woman graphically humping away on the forest floor, with the words "Look at those animals!" scrolling across the bottom. I dialed up the internet. If I knew more about Jason's current girlfriend, I might have a better idea of what she was doing here.

Fortunately, we all left a trail. It took me forty-five minutes of searching the online archives of Niagara County's newspapers—the *Gazette*, *Sun*, and *Democrat*—to find what I hadn't known I was looking for: an obituary for Regina Krupps, the woman who'd lost the original diamond necklace.

She'd died three weeks earlier.

There was no photo accompanying the obituary, and the information was short and sweet: "Regina Krupps, age 104, died of heart failure in her home in Niagara Falls. Her husband, noted entrepreneur Bradford Krupps, preceded Mrs. Krupps in death. Mr. and Mrs. Krupps, along with their dear friends the Phillip Carnegie family, created the Niagara County Center for the Arts in 1940. She was attended at her death by her nurse of four years and survived by her beloved bichon frise, Berry Blossom."

Bull's-eye.

I'll *bet* her nurse attended her, and I had a hairy feeling that nurse was in town, rooming with Jason at Shangri-La and borrowing the last name Krupps. It was just too much to believe that she and Jason had coincidentally arrived in town all the way from Niagara County, New York, at the same time everyone and their dog was looking for a lost diamond necklace. It was much more likely that the nurse had had reason to believe she could find "a pile of rocks" at Shangri-La, though she must not know exactly where to look, or she'd already be gone.

I printed out a copy of the obituary and walked out to find Gina snoring on the couch, the corners of her mouth still greasy. I pulled off her shoes, covered her with a quilt, and was out the door.

I took the back roads all the way to my house, and the sweet, dusty smell of gravel in June filled my car. I was in a good mood, which only increased when I spotted the package waiting on my front steps. I ripped it open right then and there and discovered my Z-Force inside, battery included. It looked a little smaller than in the picture, but it wasn't the first time I'd been disappointed by size. I recovered quickly because the stun gun looked fierce in my hand, and it had a good weight, like a heavy flashlight. I hooked up the nine-volt and practiced a menacing posture, zapping invisible rednecks.

My ninja moves were riling the birds, who flew from the treetops squawking. I forced myself to calm down so I didn't anger the Fowl Ones. I needed all the luck I could swing tonight. For good measure, I filled the bird feeders with sweet thistle and sunflower seeds and even nailed up a few oranges for the orioles.

There were already quite a few cars heading down the driveway I shared with Shangri-La. After a bit, the cars were replaced by people walking the mile and a half of road; there must have been no more room to park on the peninsula. After a few dozen people strolled past, I decided there'd be enough of a crowd for me to blend in, and I joined them. I rarely carried a purse, but tonight I'd dug out a medium-size, emerald-green crocheted bag from the back of my closet to hide the reassuring weight of my freshly charged zapper and to stow away any long-lost jewelry I might chance across. I took advantage of the extra room inside the purse to carry a flashlight, a skeleton key that I'd scored at a rummage sale, and some gum.

As I approached the resort grounds, the sun was setting on the west side of Whiskey. The light was spectacular, slicing through trees and casting people into backlit shadows. The general feel of the crowd was light, and there was joking and laughter. I heard talk of fireworks later, but much of the conversation centered on the fake body found in the lake. I fell in with a small group in their late forties or early fifties, all of them dressed like out-of-town golfers.

The short, broad man I was directly behind spoke. "Gawd, I'd hate to be the idiot who found that stuffed dive suit. I heard whoever it was nearly crapped herself."

My fingers itched to grab the zapper. Dang tourists, judging me. I bet I could bump up against this guy and drop him without taking my hand out of my purse. I slipped closer, my eyes pasted on his comb-over.

"Doesn't take Einstein to tell a human body from a stuffed wet suit!" he said, laughing.

Two more feet and I'd reach his backside. As I cradled the black zapper inside my purse, I wondered how much of a buffer his shorts would provide him.

"Let's hope the ditz doesn't have a driver's license! Probably can't tell a stop sign from a tree."

One more step. All I had to do was zap and blend back in the crowd. It'd be a gratifying way to begin tonight's festivities.

He was on a roll. "I hope she buys a flashlight so she can find her ass to shit."

Half a step. I hit the on button and felt a soft hum of electricity. I leaned in, hypnotized by the rhythm of his large rear cheeks rolling one over the other like ships on the storm of his thighs.

Crack! The loud boom shocked me, and I dropped the stun gun into my purse, my hand releasing the button. Green and gold lights burned in the sky, competing with the setting sun for attention, and sparkled down to Earth like crashing fireflies. The crowd around me stopped and oohed.

I walked past the group I had been tailing, glaring at the guy who'd been knocking me. He smiled appreciatively at my rear end before returning his attention to the sky.

That dude didn't know how lucky he was.

Chapter 16

Children were screaming and chasing one another as a last firework shot out from the public access and over the peninsula. Apparently, the blasts were just meant to announce the party.

All around, people were mingling and smiling, drinks in hand as they rode the excitement of outdoor entertainment on a warm summer evening. The theater troupe was providing preshow distractions in the only clearing on the grounds. A juggler danced around the tiki torches lighting the natural stage, a unicycling clown pedaled back and forth to the delighted glee of the kids watching, and a man in a tuxedo tossed candy from stilt level. Two short figures dressed as Tweedledum and Tweedledee rolled around on the ground, and I couldn't tell from my spot if they were small adults or children.

A tropical theme blended in with the circus feel of the Romanov entertainment, leftovers from the resort's annual Memorial Day tiki party. Bongo players dressed in grass skirts and leis pounded a tribal beat on the stage's periphery, and dancers swayed around them. The mingling of the tropics with carnival was unsettling, like interspecies mating. I wondered how much this spectacle cost and how the Gibsons were paying for it.

There'd been no cover charge, and only a handful of people here were paying guests. For the second time in as many days, I considered the possibility that the Gibsons were on the shady end of this whole diamond deal.

I sidled closer to the main stage and searched for familiar faces. I thought I spotted Jed playing one of the bongos, but the torches' flickering light made it hard to make out details.

"You need to stay close to me, and don't accept anything fried or with sugar."

I turned and spotted Peyton and Leylanda standing five feet behind me. Peyton was executing a little-girl hip wiggle to the tropical beat, her pigtails bobbing. Leylanda grasped her hand tightly.

"Hey, Peyton!" I danced my way over and we both boogied for a minute, much to Leylanda's chagrin. "Gonna be a fun night, eh?"

Leylanda stared icily at me. "Peyton, this is not fun. This is *culture*, and we are here to see a *theater* performance. Say goodbye to Ms. James."

I held out my hand, and Peyton shook it, deftly palming the Fruit Stripe gum I'd concealed there. "See you around," I said.

"See you," she chirped.

I strolled away from the center of activity and toward the front of the lodge. Samantha Krupps sat on the steps smoking a cigarette stuck in one of those long black-and-white holders that Natasha used in *Rocky and Bullwinkle*. Jason was nowhere in sight, so I strolled over.

"Hey," I said.

When she turned, it was impossible to miss her black eye, sullen and purplish under her unnaturally dark eyebrows.

"Wow, that's a nasty shiner."

"No shit."

All yesterday's chattiness was gone. I saw no reason to play at small talk. "Jason hit you?"

She dragged deep off her cigarette. Her eyes appeared hazel in the gathering night, and her dark roots seemed to glow. She scowled into the distance.

When she didn't answer, I tried another question. "Where did you say you're from?"

"I didn't."

"Niagara County, I think you said."

Her eyes flicked to me and she tensed up. I knew she wanted to look around for Jason, but she showed admirable restraint.

"Are you having a good time in Battle Lake, Samantha?"

"People call me Sam."

She was talking. I needed to keep her going as long as possible because as soon as Jason showed up, she'd shut down. "Sam, then." I smiled at her and hoped it was open and friendly. "What's there to do in Niagara County?"

"Not much, unless you like catering to tourists." She smiled without humor. "Probably a lot like living here, actually. I was a CNA for a while, a waitress here and there, sold *junk* at gift shops. You name it, I did it."

I knew from Gina that a CNA was a certified nursing assistant, and with the proper training, a CNA could be a home health aide. I decided to bluff. "I know who you took care of when you were nursing."

"You mean my aunt? So?"

Her self-assurance caught me off guard. I was certain Regina Krupps didn't have any living relatives, or they'd have been mentioned in her obituary. "She was the one who lost the diamond necklace in this lake."

Sam appeared genuinely bored as she pressed her thumb and forefinger together softly, like she was applauding the tiniest show.

I changed tack, determined to regain the upper hand. "How'd you meet Jason?"

Sam took a final puff on her cigarette and ground it into the side of the stairs. She started to insert another one in her holder, then tossed her holder into the bushes and slapped the cigarette straight in her mouth. "He strolled into a shop I was working at. We sold wedding packages, sort of like Vegas, and he had a horse-faced redhead on his arm. He took one look at me and left her." She laughed icily. "Aren't I lucky?"

I ignored the question. "Why'd you travel out here?"

"To meet Jason's family." She fidgeted, dodging the question and my eyes.

"You and Jason do any diving since you got here?"

She took a deep drag. "Ha! You couldn't get me to go in a lake to save a baby. If I can't see the bottom, I don't get wet."

That jolted me. I assumed Jason had rented three sets of gear for himself and Sam, with one set left over for the fake body. If she didn't dive, Jason had an accomplice who was probably a lot scarier than her.

Suddenly, a cold hand grabbed my neck, and every thought dropped out of my head as I was transported back into the water, drowning. I squealed, and the hand let go. I whipped around to face the oily smile of the ringmaster, who, dressed as a lion tamer, had handed me the Romanov flyer in the Senior Sunset lobby the other day.

"We need a lovely lady to help us get this show started," he hissed, directing me toward the stage, "and you'll do perfectly." As he held up a decorated cane, the music screeched to a halt and all eyes turned to us. Talk about not blending into a crowd. I could be naked and in flames and be less obvious.

"Ladies and gentlemen!" His voice carried across the grounds. "Welcome to the world-renowned Romanov Traveling Theater!"

On cue, the bongo players sprinkled throughout the crowd started slapping their skins in a slow and steady rhythm while chanting a low "Hiya, ha hiya."

"Tonight, we have a rare treat for you! In addition to the enticing entertainment provided by our peninsula performers, you will get a preview of the local production of William C. Shakespeare's *The Taming of the Shrew!*"

William *C.*? Hadn't it been William *S.* before? Who were these Romanovs? It was now fully dark beyond the circle of tiki-torch light, and I tried to slink away into the inkiness. The ringmaster snatched me back.

"This beatific lady has agreed to take part in our opening extravaganza by starring in our disappearing act! Young lady, have we met before?"

I nodded.

"The lady says no! This is our first meeting! Peninsula assistants, please bring out the Vanishing Box."

There was a somber drumroll, and two of the skirt-clad bongo players hoisted a heavy box to the center of the earthen stage. The container was about five and a half feet tall, and from a distance, I imagine it looked ornate. Up close, I could see it was covered in cheap plastic designed to look like carved wood. There was a door on the front without a doorknob. The ringmaster tapped it with his cane, and it opened. He stepped inside, crouching, and then out to show that it was a real box, and pounded the sides to demonstrate it was solid.

"Assistants, please lead our lovely volunteer inside!"

I was starting to panic. Public speaking was bad, but public disappearing was worse.

The bongo players grabbed my wrists and dragged me toward the box as I dug in my heels. I couldn't reach my stun gun and felt like a character in a Shirley Jackson story as the crowd hooted and hollered in glee. I turned to beg the bongo players to let me go and saw Jed grinning dopily at me.

"Jed!" I hissed. "What are you doing in a skirt, and why the *hell* don't you let me go!"

"Easy money, Mira, and don't worry." His grin struck me as dopier than usual. "This is a cool trick. I got to do it once in rehearsal today. You'll be fine, dude. Just play along."

I relaxed not at all but gave up fighting as they shoved me into the box. The front closed like a coffin door, and the ringmaster's voice became muffled. The inside of the box smelled like sweat and vinegar. I had to crouch down, my knees and shoulders scraping the cheap wood.

"I will say the magic words, tap three times on the box, and show you our lovely volunteer has disappeared! Abracov, dabrocov, Romanov!"

There were three taps, but I'm sure I was the only one who heard them over the deafening cracks of a fresh round of fireworks. Without warning, I was jerked out the back of the box as shards of light exploded overhead. Four hands shoved me into a container just big enough to hold me in the fetal position, and I felt myself being carried off. There was sufficient space to breathe but not enough to struggle. Fortunately, my hand had been clutching my purse when I was thrust into the tight jail, and I concentrated on working it inside.

I was sweating with the exertion of small movements by the time my fingertips brushed against the solid plastic of my little soldier. I grabbed on to it, determined to force some involuntary bodily functions out of whoever was transporting me as soon as they released me.

If they released me.

Clearly, reappearing wasn't an integral part of this disappearing act.

Chapter 17

My breathing grew harsh as the sounds of the party faded, and my muscles screamed to break free. I considered yelling, but my voice would be drowned out by the exterior noise. There was only one way to walk off Shangri-La—the strip of road that was the driveway—which meant there was now water on either side of me. I didn't want to give anyone a reason to dump me in it. Maybe this was just a harmless magic trick and I'd be released as soon as I was totally out of the audience's sight.

I concentrated on getting my breathing under control, trying to draw comfort from the familiar smell of Whiskey Lake and the surrounding woods. I was almost calm when the reverberations of road were suddenly replaced by the rustling of brush. They were carting me into the woods! To do what?

A scream was building in my throat when the jostling stopped, and I was set down gently. The front of the container was opened.

"Du—"

I leaped and zapped wildly, managing to connect with both of the carriers at least once. I stared wildly from Jed's crumpling face to the slumped body of the other bongo player. I recognized him from the bait shop. He'd sold me a newspaper and Lemonheads last week and asked me how I liked the weather.

I forced myself to blink and breathe, but it felt like I was getting attacked from every direction. No, that wasn't right. I'd been listening to the footfalls. It was just the three of us in the woods, and two of us were currently rump-to-stars on the forest floor.

I took in the two elm trees in front of me knotted together like lovers, the now-faint hum of the crowd on Shangri-La, and the whisper of breeze in the treetops. I was stiff from my temporary confinement. I glanced over to see what I'd been hauled here in. It was a bongo drum, a little bigger than the rest, with a side that opened out. It had probably been modified just for this trick.

I leaned over and felt Jed's pulse and then his friend's. They were both a little rapid but strong. I considered sticking around to apologize, but then thought better of it. Both guys were probably so high that this zapping wouldn't even register. Besides, everyone knew it wasn't cool to transport a chick to the woods in a carrier disguised as a bongo drum without letting her in on the plan.

I jogged back toward the road and the party on Shangri La. When I reached the edge of the woods, I slid off my tennies, laced them over my shoulder, and dropped down to the water's edge. I stuck to the edge of the slough side of the lake, my feet sinking in the swampy ground. I envisioned leeches hanging off my toes like spaghetti noodles. It was gross, but being quiet was more important than being bloodsucker-free.

My plan was to make sure Sam and Jason were in the crowd, then sneak into the lodge and up to the main bedroom. I estimated that I could be in and out in under five minutes. I likely had more time than that since whoever had an interest in my whereabouts had already done their best to get rid of me and wouldn't be expecting me back so soon, if at all.

I peered through feathery weeping willow branches at the frenzy of the Romanov show, the tiki torches vividly lighting the scene and ensuring my invisibility in the shadows. I couldn't see what was happening onstage, but the audience was crowded ten deep. I spotted Sam leaning against a tree apart from the crowd, her cigarette holder in place again, smoking and looking pensive. It took me a while to find Jason, but it was worth the effort. He stood about fifty feet from me and on the other side of the crowd from Sam, looking monstrously uncomfortable.

And it was immediately clear why.

A bedecked Kennie was leaning into him, her hand on his upper thigh.

She was talking animatedly, and every swing of her arms promised to release one of the mammoth breasts shoved into the black rubber of her tank top. Her natural hair was buried under the red, green, and yellow braids of extensions, and she wore a tie-dyed skirt. Her red lipstick and green and yellow eye shadow complemented the cacophony of color. This was clearly her effort to attract a younger man, and I applauded it. No woman, no cry.

I swallowed bubbling laughter. I didn't have much time. Sticking to the shadows, I sneaked into the lodge through the darkened kitchen in back. I made my way up the servants' stairs, fishing in my purse for the skeleton key I'd brought with me. I had the wild idea that it might work in a house as old as this one as long as all the original locks were intact.

I reached the second floor and made my way to the massive main bedroom, placing my hand on the cool crystal doorknob, and was startled when it swung open.

"Hello?" I whispered.

There was no answer, so I traded the skeleton key for the stun gun and my penlight and tiptoed in. Moonlight spilled across the carpet, illuminating a major mess and a minor carpentry project.

The whole room stank of sweat and fried food. The bed was unmade and strewn with clothes, there were empty Coors Light bottles and Styrofoam take-out boxes scattered on the floor, and all the furniture had been moved to the far side of the room. It looked like a rock band had stopped by, but the main room wasn't as shocking as the closet. The door had been taken off its hinges and the interior was ripped apart. It was as if a hundred razor-toothed beavers had gone at it—the paneling was displaced, the wallpaper hung in strips, and there were holes sawed out of the Sheetrock.

This crude destruction had paid off, because in the back of the far-right corner of the closet was an opening about three feet high and two feet wide. There was probably a switch that would have tripped the miniature door to open, but a crowbar had done this dirty work. My heart was flirting with my stomach, and they both agreed I should get my ass in on this discussion and go home to relative safety. After all, I'd already been disappeared once tonight; I was sure there were people around who wouldn't mind making that permanent. Yet I couldn't fight the feeling, like fizzy bubbles dancing in my veins, that if I stayed, I'd discover treasure way bigger than any rhinestone I'd ever hidden.

I aimed the flashlight beam into the space, dropping to my knees for a better view. My light revealed a shallow, long room that went deeper than I could see. The architect who planned this place must have devised it so that the secret room was invisible from the outside. I leaned in farther, and my flashlight reflected off a metal structure that looked vaguely familiar. It took me a few seconds to place it. I had seen a similar contraption on a rerun of *The Beverly Hillbillies* in which Jethro had been making moonshine.

I bet I was looking at how Whiskey Lake had earned its nickname.

I crouched and squeezed myself into the hidden room. The floor had been dusty at one point, but a lot of footprints had flurried that. I ran my hands along the cool metal of the still and flashed my light up at the shelving that lined the back wall. There were hundreds of bottles stored on the shelves, and they all appeared empty.

Immediately behind the still were two small white tanks that looked newer than everything else, along with some glass tubes like the ones we used in middle-school science class. One of the tanks had "anhydrous ammonia" written on the side, and the other looked like a compact gas tank for a propane grill. I knew farmers used the ammonia around here to fertilize their corn, but I had no idea why it would be stored in this room next to a tank of gas for a grill. One thing was clear, though: Jason hadn't yet found what he was looking for in this room, or he'd be gone.

Shirly had said other guests had reported missing jewelry that summer, not just Regina. I'd assumed he must have caught Regina stealing or hiding jewelry when he walked in on her in the closet. Now I wondered if instead she'd stumbled across the moonshining operation and whoever had been running it. If it'd been employees running the still, getting them all fired would have given her free rein over it. Or, if the Addamses were moonshining, she could have blackmailed them after she stumbled across their operation, which would explain why they'd sold the place shortly after her visit and why they weren't mentioned in her obituary along with the Carnegies.

I knew my time was running out. Sam and Jason could return at any minute, and I needed to find what they'd somehow missed. It looked like they'd gone over everything with a fine-tooth but greasy comb. Neither of them were neat people, though, and dirty people often didn't acknowledge the world below knee level. I dropped to all fours and ran my hand along the bottom of everything—the still, the shelves, an old typewriter. I was almost ready to give up when I snagged some material secured underneath the shelf farthest from the entrance.

I pulled a purple silk bag loose, amazed at the fabric's softness despite its obvious age. Inside were four mothballs and a rolled parchment about six inches long, tied into a tube with a strip of leather. I was pulling at the leather when the bedroom door opened and then slammed shut.

My mouth and anus echoed the gesture.

I quickly switched off the flashlight, hoping it hadn't been spotted, and shoved the parchment into the bag and the bag into my purse. I considered hiding based on my memory of this now-dark room, but I discarded that as stupid. It was only a matter of time until Jason and his mystery accomplice came back here, and judging by the two feet of Sheetrock, insulation, and wood I'd crawled through to get in, this space was soundproof. It would be pretty easy to do away with me. After all, this secret chamber had gone undisturbed for almost seventy years. I was in no hurry to rot in here for another seventy.

At least if I sneaked back into the bedroom, I could make a mad dash to the door and yell for help if I didn't make it. And who knew? It might just be Sam out there. I could take her down. I pulled out my stun gun and swore I'd name my first child after it if it got me out of here. This would all be a suspenseful bedtime story I'd tell little Z-Force someday.

I inched my way toward the opening, relieved when whoever was in the bedroom flipped on a light. I could now make out the faint shapes of the stills and shelves. I crawled past them, leaning toward the exit hole without peeking out so I could take stock of my surroundings.

"She's the goddamn mayor, Sammie," Jason was saying. "What, am I supposed to be rude to her?"

My stomach dropped. I wasn't going to be able to slip out of here easily.

Sam made a scoffing noise. "How about keeping your tongue out of her throat? Would that be too damn rude?"

The corner of my mouth twitched. *Kennie and Jason, sitting in a tree, kay-eye-ess-ess-eye-en-gee . . .*

Jason's voice became soft, pleading. "Baby doll, you know you're the only one I want to kiss. Come over here to Daddy."

I heard the bedsprings creak, followed by a deep, resigned sigh. "I gotta pee first. Why don't you clean up some of this mess? You live like a damn pig."

The bathroom door closed. Seconds later, I heard what sounded like a racehorse emptying its bladder. Jason, meanwhile, began his version of cleaning. I heard the telltale zip of jeans and the sound of clothes hitting the floor.

"Hurry up, baby! Little Jason ain't got all day."

The bathroom door opened again. "Baby, it doesn't take Little Jason longer than all of three minutes, so quit your bitchin'."

Score one for the lady.

The light flicked off, sending me back into darkness, only it wasn't so black now that I wasn't deep inside the secret room. I waited until

I heard the creaks of another body joining Jason on the bed. I crawled out of the secret room and into the regular closet. The bed was to the right and out of sight of my position, but I had a straight shot to the door, four feet to my left. I grimaced when the springs started squawking rhythmically. Sam hadn't been lying about Jason's speed-racer love.

I fought the urge to stand and run. Speed would draw too much attention, and if Jason saw me, he'd hunt me down to the ends of the earth. I sucked in a deep breath and forced myself to move as slowly as a turtle. The room was submerged in shadow, and I kept my head straight down to minimize movement as I inched toward the door. Out of the corner of my eye, Sam was riding Jason like a ten-cent pony outside the drugstore. Shuddering, I filed it all away under TOP SECRET—DON'T OPEN AGAIN.

By keeping my movements slow and disciplined, I made it to the front door in under a minute. I snaked up the wall and slid my hand toward the doorknob. It was crystal on this side, too. I had my face to the wall with my back to the room, vulnerable.

That's when the heaving on the bed stopped.

I panicked, ripped open the door, and ran. I heard yelling behind me, but I was taking the stairs three at a time. I burst out the main door before Jason would have time to yank his pants on. There was still a crowd gathered, but it looked like the show was winding down.

My goal was to get as far away as I could, as fast as I could.

When the crowd parted, I ran.

I made it ten feet before I heard a pop like a firecracker at the same time a fiery blow to the center of my forehead knocked me flat.

Chapter 18

"It's a shooting! Somebody's been shot!"

People started screaming and moving back. I lay there, paralyzed, in agony. I'd taken a bullet to the head.

I was dying.

A warm trickle bled into one of my eyes. I put my hand up, my mind scraped blank with terror. Why wasn't anyone helping me? As if reading my mind, a walkie-talkie crackled, and then someone yelled out that the resort owners were calling 911.

More than anything, I didn't want to touch the hole in my head, but I couldn't stop myself. I put my fingers on the spot about an inch above my eyebrows and was repulsed at the hard and wet blob protruding there. Were my brains leaking out? Morbid curiosity won over prudence. I gingerly lifted the blob of bulging flesh, tipping my eyes so I could see it. The pain didn't get any worse, so I tried to focus on the blob.

I blinked, and then blinked again.

I was holding a squashed June bug.

I had not been shot. In my rush to escape Jason, I'd collided with a flying beetle with such force that I'd juiced it right on my own noggin.

I sat up shakily to tell the crowd the ambulance wouldn't be needed, that the professional dork who'd almost drowned herself on a fake dead body yesterday had now just knocked herself silly on a June bug the size of a crow. That's when I realized that the crowd wasn't gathering around me, and the ambulance hadn't been called for my sake.

Somebody really had been shot.

Chapter 19

Brushing bug juice off my tender forehead, I pulled myself up and pushed through the mob circled around one of the last tiki torches still burning. The raucous sounds of partying had been replaced by the buzzing hum of panic. In the middle of the circle lay the performer dressed as Tweedledee.

He had indeed been an adult and was now an adult with a pool of blood gathering under his small body. Kellie Gibson was by his side, searching for a pulse.

He wasn't moving.

A screaming ambulance charged up the narrow road to Shangri-La. The crowd stepped back so the EMTs could access the fallen performer. While they loaded him onto the gurney, I turned to the guy next to me. "What happened?"

He appeared dazed. He kept getting jostled by the crowd, both those trying to squeeze in for a better look and those trying to leave. "That crazy ringmaster shot him! He shot him and then disappeared into that black box! Jesus, what sort of show is this?"

I wondered the same thing.

The happy peninsula party was now a chaos of performers, police, and blood. Chief Wohnt plowed through the crowd and barked orders, but otherwise, the throng was a panicked blur. The paramedics cleared a path, and I realized that the carnival performers were melting into the dark. By the time the stretcher reached the ambulance, the only people left in the light were Battle Lake natives.

Why wouldn't the performers be gathered around one of their own? Were they going after the ringmaster? If so, I had an inside edge. I knew where the black box emptied out at. I pushed through the people who now rushed to leave like lemmings. A number of children were crying, and parents were pushing strollers through the grass in their hurry to escape.

The police were cordoning off the area, and it looked like it was going to be a long night of questioning witnesses. I skirted into the shadows and left the way I'd come, along the swampy slough side. I traveled unnoticed to the edge of the woods where I'd been dumped, stopping to worry momentarily about poison ivy. There was a bumper crop this year. Chances were good, I'd already stepped through it.

When I reached the drop-off location, I saw that I was too late. Jed and his fellow zappee must have recovered and left. There was a second bongo next to the one I'd been carried in, its front open to reveal an empty hidey hole.

The murderous ringmaster had escaped.

I decided on the spot that I would sleep at Gina's tonight, right after I reached a lighted area where I could look at what was written on the parchment I'd lifted from the secret room. The anticipation was killing me, but I needed to get far away from Jason and Shangri-La first.

I jogged to my car, locked all the doors with my sweaty hands, and drove to Chip's Bait in town. There, under the flickering glow of the parking-lot light, hands trembling, I untied the leather strip and rolled the parchment open with all the anticipation of a lover opening a Valentine's Day gift. The movement released the scent of mothballs.

The paper was so thick it felt handmade, and the blue-black ink had bled through. The writing was still legible, however. It read:

Jvgu lbhe onpx gb gur xvffvat gerr jnyx frira fgrcf abegujrfg xarry 23 yrsg 12 evtug 11 yrsg.

My stomach dropped. I'd been hoping to find a map with a big red X over a sparkly Richie Rich drawing of diamonds. This was a message in a foreign code with regular numbers. I slapped my steering wheel in frustration. There was nothing more I could do with this tonight.

Tomorrow, I would bring it to Battle Lake's resident code cracker to see what he could puzzle out.

Chapter 20

I woke up one hour past sunrise after an uneasy sleep. Pushing myself up from Gina's crusty couch, I gently touched the lump the size of a crab apple dead center on my forehead and acknowledged a headache of Mardi Gras proportions. I stumbled into her bathroom, showered, and felt slightly worse. I needed coffee, ibuprofen, and a talk with Ron Sims, the county crossword-puzzle champion. He took words as seriously as a heart attack, and if he couldn't unscramble the puzzle I'd found, no one could.

While I was in the newspaper's office, I needed to also access the *Recall*'s archives to find out what the paper had reported about the diamond necklace and Mrs. Krupps back when it all happened. A second visit to Shirly Tolverson might be in order as well. What I'd discovered in that secret room last night confirmed that he'd done some shrewd editing of his Shangri-La story.

I hoped I could accomplish all this before I needed to open the library at ten.

I wrapped myself in a towel and stepped gingerly out of the bathroom, trying to hold my tender head completely still on my neck. Gina was sitting on the couch in the living room. "Hey, G, you have any aspirin?"

It took me a second to realize that she shouldn't be home at this time of day; she should be three hours into her grueling shift. Another beat later, I realized that she was crying.

"He's cheating."

I sucked in a loud breath. "What?"

"Leif. He's cheating on me."

I dropped down next to her and threw my arm around her shoulders. Leif had seemed to take his marriage for granted, but I'd never clocked him for a cheater. "How do you know?"

Gina stared at the floor, her face red and swollen. Her hair was corralled into a scrunchie, and she wore a tattered brown bathrobe with old-fashioned grandma pajamas underneath. Her voice cracked when she spoke. "He told me. He said he needed to come clean with me because our relationship is so important."

I scowled at the weak logic of a guilty man. You didn't earn a medal for being an honest cheater. "I'm sorry, sweetie. Who's it with?"

"He wouldn't give me a name. Some ice-fishing siren, I suppose. I knew I should have gone out with him when he asked. It's just so damn boring." She threw her head back, shaking tendrils of yellow hair loose from their tie, and sobbed like a three-year-old. I let her, even though every bellow dragged through my bug-bashed head like a rusty fishhook. When she calmed down, I asked her what she was going to do.

She sniffled what sounded like a bucket of snot and reached for the box of Kleenex. "What can I do, Mira? I love him. He's my husband. We're together for better or worse."

Her words ignited a sudden white anger in me. That had been my mother's attitude during her entire tumultuous marriage to my father—*he's my husband. I have to stay.*

There was a misconception that bad people walked around with knives and guns, kicking nuns, taking candy from babies, cussing, visible horns on their heads. But the truth was that bad people looked just like the rest of us. They could bring you flowers on your birthday or call you to find out how your interview went or show up unexpectedly at your basketball game. Then, when you were fooled into relaxing, they'd get pass-out drunk on the regular or have sex with a stranger after they'd pledged their heart to you.

I believed that when someone showed their true colors, and those colors were primarily a cheaty gray, you needed to respond accordingly: cut them out of your life.

Gina, with her runny nose, puffy eyes, and broken heart, didn't want to hear my theory on bad people—I was sure of that. She wanted her husband to love her like mad. "Well, G, if you're going to stick it out, take advantage of your current position."

"Huh?" Another snort into her squelchy tissue.

"He's got his tail between his legs, so ask for what you need right now. Get him to agree to marriage counseling and to take you out for a nice night at a fancy restaurant, if nothing else."

Her soggy green eyes stared into mine. "It can work, can't it? People can move past this stuff, right?"

"Anything is possible." I grimaced. "Now, I'm sorry, but I need some ibuprofen before my head cracks off and rolls under the couch."

Gina provided the pills, Sid and Nancy gave me a coffee and cinnamon scone on the house after they saw my green-and-purple forehead ("No shit. A June bug?"), and by the time I met up with Ron at the *Recall* office, I felt marginally human. The office still smelled like ink and the walls were still tan, but something in the room hinted at excitement. This was a good time to own a newspaper in Battle Lake.

"Mira James! Just the person I was looking for. I've got two stories for you to write. Shoot, we might need a special edition!"

The ibuprofen had fully kicked in, and the caffeine was pleasantly stroking my serotonin. Gina's sadness had painted a shadow on the day, but I couldn't do anything for her right now.

"Fine," I said, rolling the parchment out on his desk. "But first, I need help with a puzzle. What language does this look like to you?"

He glanced over the top of his bifocals. "English."

I scowled. "In case you haven't noticed, I am somewhat familiar with the predominant language of North America. This isn't English."

"It's a cryptogram, James. Substitution cipher. Look at the numbers, syntax, and primary repetition of letters. Third-grade stuff. Now, if you want a real challenge, what you do is pull out the Saturday *New York Times* puzzle and settle back for a full, sweaty day of word wrestling. I remember—"

"Can you unjumble it?"

"Do fat men make the best lovers?"

For crying in the night! I hated trick questions. I copied the code onto his pink "While You Were Out" pad and returned the original to the silk wrap. "Just tell me what this says, okay?"

"Business before pleasure, James. Since you're our resident homicide writer, I want you to find out what you can about the man who was shot last night at Shangri-La. I need the scoop on him—his name, where he was from, how long he's been with the traveling theater, how he's doing—"

I wiped off my coffee mustache. "You mean he's still alive?"

"Last I heard over the police radio. His heart was still beating when they brought him to Lake Region, anyhow." Ron smacked his desk. "I need that article ASAP. Also, Gary Wohnt dropped off this press release. Make sure it's clean before we run it."

I glanced at the paper Ron shoved in my hand. It was short and typed in an austere, sans serif font with zero formatting:

UNDERAGE FIELD DRINKIING DOWN 43%

Otter Tail County teenagers are imbibing in local corn and soybean fields 43% less than they were a year ago. "We have only received three complaints about teenagers drinking in fields, down from seven this time last year," according to Battle Lake police chief Gary Wohnt. "We attribute the decrease in outdoor, underage partying to the increase in random patrols, the

DARE campaign, and the Olsen boys going off to college."

The Battle Lake Police Department will continue to focus on fields as a source of trouble but will expand their efforts to parked cars, abandoned silos, and public beaches after hours.

This was my life. I needed to fact-check an article on field drinking, rural Minnesota's favorite youth activity, and write an article on a traveling actor who'd been shot. Just another day at the office.

"If I do this, you'll solve the puzzle?" I asked. When Ron's brow furrowed, I said, "I'll throw in fresh hot scones from the Fortune for a full week."

He nodded and waved without looking up at me, his head buried in the puzzle and his glasses threatening to fall off his nose. "I need another recipe, too," he grunted. "Make it a dessert this time. Too many main dishes lately."

I nodded at his bald spot, pocketed the press release, and headed to the back room. The *Recall* had been around since the early 1900s. Ron'd paid big bucks to have a California-based document-scanning business convert all the microfiche archives to searchable PDF file format. That meant that I'd be able to complete the background investigation I should have done on Shangri-La and its main players from the moment I'd been handed the story.

I fired up the Mac and searched editions from the 1920s. Back then, the paper came out only once a month, and it was mostly filled with crop information and sensational stories on the dangers of immigrants and Indians. I was surprised by the amount of photos and advertisements, mostly for radios. An October 1923 ad promised to provide "a radio that can catch the waves out of Yankton, South Dakota!"

The August 1924 issue of the *Recall* featured a full page on the Shangri-La construction project, but it didn't tell me anything new. It wasn't until the June 1929 issue that I hit pay dirt—an article on the suspicious disappearance of jewelry at the Addamses' house. It listed these missing items: a Victorian lava cameo bracelet; two hematite intaglio rings; a coral, platinum, and diamond double-clip brooch; a black pearl sautoir; two sapphire, seven emerald, and twelve diamond rings; assorted diamond earrings; a diamond and emerald tiara; and a diamond pendant necklace.

I whistled. That was quite a haul, and I didn't even know what a sautoir was. If the thief was half as good at stashing jewelry as I was, Shangri-La was lousy with hidden bling.

I dug in my purse for paper to copy the list on. I shut down the computer and made for the door, hollering at Ron as I passed him, "You call the minute you get that solved. Fresh scones . . ."

His head was still down in the puzzle. "Go! I'm not paying you to nag me!"

I paused. "Please. You couldn't get a high school kid to work the fryer at the Dairy Queen for what you pay me. Call me, okay?"

"I'll call," he said. "If I don't get bogged down with more work, expect to have this solved within the hour."

Chapter 21

I stepped into the blinding light of Main Street and yanked my gas-station-rack sunglasses over my eyes. It was nine fifteen in the morning, and I wasn't sure where to go next. I wanted to talk to Shirly and ferret out what he'd omitted from his Shangri-La story, and I needed to interview Gary Wohnt, but I had only forty-five minutes until I was supposed to open the library. I shirked certain areas of my life, like forming relationships with other humans and occasionally personal hygiene, but I had a strong work ethic.

I decided to visit the Sunset first, because I could always phone Chief Wohnt for the information I needed. Shirly, however, I needed to talk to in person. I wanted to be able to read his face.

Battle Lake had one central street, so everything was technically around the corner from something else. It would take me all of six minutes to walk to the nursing home. On the way, I passed six Ford and five Dodge pickups plus a crowd gathering in the First National Bank parking lot. Families came out in droves for the turtle races, held every Tuesday during the summer months. A bank employee was hosing down the already-steaming pavement so the creatures didn't melt their little mitts right into the black tar while loads of brightly clothed kids painted numbers on their turtles' backs.

I spotted Peyton standing alone off to the side of the crowd, wearing a bright-pink sundress and matching hat, her pigtails poking out from the bottom. I waved. She gave me a happy two-handed wave in return. I was not surprised to see her turtle-free. Technically, they were dirty creatures with a tendency to pee like a river when alarmed. Leylanda wouldn't allow Peyton to touch one. I was actually surprised she wasn't presently hovering over her daughter. *She must be within nagging distance.*

I scanned the crowd and was shocked to discover her talking animatedly with Jason in the shade of the bank. Seeing him made it feel like I had cement hardening in my stomach. He'd buzzed off his hair between last night and now, and the severe cut drew attention to his dark, restless eyes.

I instinctively ducked behind a Ford F-150 and watched the two interact. Leylanda was laughing, and he ogled her boobs whenever she tossed her head back to giggle. I hadn't known they knew each other, though it made sense since they'd both grown up in Battle Lake. Were they hooking up? They didn't seem to have much in common, but I knew Jason could be charming when he wanted, and Leylanda might be lonely. She was divorced, her husband long gone, and Jason considered himself single no matter who he was seeing.

I was too far away to hear what they were talking about, but their faces changed as they both glanced toward Jason's crotch. They must have been reacting to a noise, because he pulled his cell phone out of his pocket and stuck it to his ear.

He turned away from Leylanda whip fast.

I was the only one who saw how dark and still his face became as he continued the phone conversation. Abruptly, he jerked the cell from his ear, fished in his front pants pocket, pulled out a few green bills, and handed them to Leylanda, who stood directly behind him. He pointed across the street at Granny's Pantry. Leylanda made a motion toward Peyton, who was watching the turtle races hypnotically.

Jason waved his hand in an "It'll be fine" manner and turned away again, effectively dismissing her. Leylanda watched him uncertainly, glanced back at Granny's Pantry, and then back at Peyton. Her struggle was painfully clear. She wanted to be a mom who could run across the street, let her daughter out of sight for a few moments to buy her candy, and bring it back, but it went against everything she believed in.

She finally made up her mind and speed walked to Granny's, moving as fast as she could without running.

Jason, for his part, strode stiffly to the rear of the parking lot. The kiddie crowd cheered as the first turtle crossed the line, which was when Peyton broke out of her trance and looked around. She didn't see her mom, so she skipped over to Jason, who had his back to her and the crowd as he continued his animated phone conversation. Meanwhile, Leylanda ran into and popped out of Granny's in record time. She must have grabbed whatever was closest to the door, thrown her money at the cash register, and dashed out.

That minute was probably the longest Peyton had ever been out of Leylanda's sight. As soon as Peyton spotted her mom, she darted from Jason's side to grab for the candy store bag. I couldn't see Peyton's face, but I imagine she was miserably disappointed when she pulled out the red apple. I didn't even know Granny's sold fruit. It should be illegal for a candy and ice cream shop to sell healthy things. Was nothing sacred?

Jason clicked his phone shut, and even from a distance, I could feel the rage pouring off him. He must have received really bad news. He started to scan the crowd, which was my cue to leave. I curved my shoulders and hunched down, copying Leylanda's speed walk as I hurried toward the library.

I made it a block before his brawny hand clamped down on my shoulder, making me jump like a squirrel.

Chapter 22

"Hello, Mira."

I shrugged off his paw and tried to walk away, but he wrapped his arm around my waist and dragged me behind Milner's Dentistry in a vicious two-step. I glanced back at the turtle races, but no one was facing our direction save a wistful-looking Leylanda. I considered yelling for help, but I was pretty sure Jason wouldn't hurt me in public, and I didn't want to scare the kids.

"I saw you made it to the show last night," he hissed into my ear.

I shoved myself away from him. "I saw you, too. It looked like you and Kennie were having a blast. Are you going steady, or was it just a heat-of-the-moment thing?"

He swelled up like a premenstrual salt lick, his fingers twitching at his sides. Then, just like that, he was calm, his tone amused. "Yeah, that was funny. I'm glad the guys didn't see me with her. I'd never hear the end of it, being hit on by a nasty skank like Kennie Rogers."

I was speechless. Suddenly, I was talking with the even-tempered Jason that Sunny called one of her best friends. Hello, Jekyll and Hyde.

"Say, Mira, funniest thing." He laughed here to illustrate his point, a warm, companionable sound that made my lips twitch against my better judgment. "Someone took something very special from me last night. Could you help me find it?"

I was certain Jason hadn't seen me clearly when I fled his room, so I had nothing to lose by acting helpful now. "Sure. Drop by the library later to tell me how I can help. Really, though, man, I need to go."

When I turned to leave, he snatched the purse from my shoulder. I grabbed at it, but he was too quick. "Golly, I don't think you need to go yet." His tone was still light, mimicking mine, but his eyes were sharp and black, his pupils eerily swollen in the light.

A flash of fear jolted me. I was in danger.

The tied parchment was on the top. He grabbed it easily and chuckled, tossing my crocheted purse to the ground. "You're a real pal, Mira. Thanks! I've been looking everywhere for this." He punched my shoulder hard enough to knock me to the ground. "Ignore the message I left at your place," he said, staring down at me. "We're cool now."

I watched his broad back turn the corner. Tears flooded my eyes as I thought about my cat and dog, vulnerable, spending the night alone. If Jason had hurt Tiger Pop or Luna, I was going to Z-Force zap him until he spoke French.

"Are you okay, honey?"

I turned quickly at the voice and wiped the tears from my eyes. "Hi, Mrs. Berns. Yeah, I just fell on the ground."

"No shit. Pretty hard to fall anywhere else." She helped me up and brushed dirt off me. "How come you're not at the library?"

"I don't feel very well." I was grateful that she ignored my tears.

"Well, give me the damn keys. I'll open her up."

"Really?"

"Honey, I raised twelve kids, ran a farm, and sewed all my own clothes. I think I can boot up a computer and scan some codes."

I had no doubt, but being fertile and good with a needle didn't necessarily translate into good public relations skills. Unfortunately, I didn't see any other option if the library was going to open on time. I handed her the keys and considered hugging her, but I needed to check on Tiger Pop and Luna, quick. I jogged back to my car, feeling tightness in the knee I'd scraped when Jason pushed me.

I sped the whole way home and raced into the house. There, my mouth went dry, my heart thudding. There was not a clean surface to be found, and it smelled like sewage and rotten fruit. The bookshelf was on its side, books torn and pages scattered. The kitchen cupboards had been ripped open, food dumped to the floor. My bedroom was the worst. The quilt and pillows were shredded, and my drawers and closets were pulled apart, clothes scattered everywhere. The bathroom wasn't as bad, but in the middle of the tub was a bear-size poop.

Jason wasn't lacking for fiber in his diet.

He clearly knew, or had assumed, it was me in the secret room last night, and he must have had an idea of what he was looking for. I wondered if he would be as disappointed with the code on the parchment as I was.

"Meow."

Really. That was how Tiger Pop said it. I ran into the laundry room, where she was stretched out in a sunbeam. I buried my face in her fur and grabbed some catnip to reward her for being alive. When Luna loped into view, my relief took my breath away. She must have been outside in her shaded house. Out of an abundance of worry, I dashed out to my garden and was relieved to see it was untouched.

Jason thought he was getting at me, but he hadn't even recognized the things that mattered. At least to me. Both animals still had dishes full of food, but I ran them fresh water and sat outside with them for a half an hour, telling them what'd transpired the past twelve hours and how happy I was that they were all right.

My fingers itched to call Mrs. Blunt and tell her that her youngest son had shit in my tub. I had no doubt she'd give him an earful, but I wanted to do more permanent damage. I cleaned up the mess, using a plastic-wrapped dustpan and broom to relocate the poop to the toilet, trying not to gag. It took three sweaty hours, but when it was all said and done, my place looked as good as new, except now I had more garbage than belongings.

I'd need to add grocery and clothes shopping to my to-do list.

I packed up Luna and Tiger Pop and dropped them off at Gina's empty house. We wouldn't be going home until Jason was behind bars. He was even more dangerous than I'd let myself believe. I felt in my bones that he was connected to the shooting at Shangri-La last night, but I needed time to prove it.

That meant I had to find the missing jewelry before he did, because he would certainly hightail it out of town once he had it in hand.

Chapter 23

After I made sure my kitty and foster dog were comfortable at Gina's, I went to the library to check on Mrs. Berns. She'd set up a table in front where she was selling kisses for a quarter and giving books away to anyone who could guess her age and weight. Fortunately, the library was slow on Tuesday mornings, even with all the fortune hunters in town, so I made the choice to run over to the Sunset before relieving her. Solving the mystery of the missing jewelry had taken on a new urgency.

I blew into the lobby, ignoring the receptionist, the smell, and the droopy old people lining the halls like skin garlands. I was happy to find Shirly in his room reading the newspaper.

"Well, hello, Ms. James!"

"Mira."

"Well, hello, Mira!" His eyes twinkled. "I hear there's some excitement going down in the outside world, most notably at Shangri-La."

"You heard right." I sized him up. He was in the same position on his bed, but now he was wearing royal-blue carpenter pants, a cream-colored polo, and red socks. His hair and smile were still impeccable. He looked quite dashing, but I caught the mischievous glint in his eyes that I'd overlooked at our last meeting.

"Remember when you told me that you caught Dolores Krupps snooping in the bedroom closet at Shangri-La?" I asked.

"Regina. Regina Krupps."

Yep, nothing wrong with his memory. "Oh, that's right. What do you think she was doing in the closet?"

"If you ask me, she was hiding the jewelry she'd been stealing since she got there."

Same thing he'd suggested the last time I was here, only with more detail. "Why would she go all the way up there to hide it? Wouldn't she be worried the Addamses would look in their own closet and come across it?"

Shirly appeared to consider this. He was the picture of thoughtful introspection. "You might be right. Maybe she was there to steal from them."

"And do you think she came across the secret room with the boot-legging operation set up in it while she was *stealing* the jewels or while she was *hiding* them?"

Shirly tensed, and then he laughed heartily. "You got a nosy streak the length of the Mississippi. How'd you know about the moonshine?"

Now we were getting somewhere. "I checked out the secret room last night. The setup is still there."

"Still there, eh? I wondered about that." He pulled himself straighter. "The room was built around it, you know. Prohibition was the scourge of the twenties, made honest men do dishonest things. The architect who built Shangri-La had a lucrative side business crafting those rum rooms."

I followed this information to its natural conclusion. "So the Addamses had him build a still into a secret room in their summer place."

Shirly smiled in a faraway manner. "No, they didn't. The architect was tired of getting a little extra money here and there for building the rum rooms. He wanted one of his own. He knew that the Addamses wouldn't be around much, and their house was going to be big enough to accommodate a hidden still. The builders knew about it, but I don't believe the Addamses ever did. During the summer season, the architect stayed away, naturally. When the place was boarded up for the winter, the hooch-making would commence. Worked great for a year, and then the architect died." He shrugged. "A few of us took it over."

That crossed one theory off the list. "I thought maybe Regina had all you guys fired and was blackmailing the Addamses because she found out about the still."

"She found the rum room, all right. Purely by accident. I caught her with a handful of jewels, digging for some more in that bedroom closet. Used to be a safe in there. When I walked in on her, I scared her so bad that she fell against the panel that opened the room.

"I told her right off that the Addamses didn't know about the moonshine. They were the nicest people and didn't need the trouble that would bring on them. Mrs. Krupps said that it would be our little secret—I wouldn't tell anyone about her sticky fingers and she wouldn't tell anyone about the liquor."

"So she lied to you?"

"Not technically. She never told the Addamses about the rum room. I imagine it was too perfect a hiding place for her loot. She did tell them that she caught *me* stealing, though, and that she thought some of the other workers were in on it. Now, remember I wasn't more than a boy, caught between two crimes: stealing and bootlegging. I figured the safest route was to keep my mouth shut and walk away."

I grimaced. "I think I know what happens next. The Addamses fire you and the others who know about the still, they reimburse the guests for the stolen jewelry, but jewelry keeps disappearing as long as Regina Krupps is staying at Shangri-La."

Shirly nodded. "Jewelry's not all. Mrs. Krupps's husband disappeared, too. I don't believe it ever made the papers. He was retired when they first visited Shangri-La, a real bastard if I'm honest, and I don't believe anyone ever missed him. Those of us who got fired joked that she hid him in the secret chamber along with the rest of her ill-gotten gains."

I shuddered at the thought. I was pretty sure I would have noticed a dead body, but I supposed a corpse could have been cut up and hidden in the still. "So why'd a rich lady need to steal?"

"You got me. I think it was one of those weird compulsions. She wasn't well in the head. She spent a lot of time arguing with herself when she thought no one was listening, and I once saw her behind a servant's cottage, hiding acorns in her mouth like a chipmunk. That woman struggled, but only sometimes. Other times, she was wicked smart. Back then, we called that sort of person 'eccentric.'"

It occurred to me that all of us struggled sometimes. I was thinking specifically of the whole year I had spent convinced that Jimmy Page was trying to contact me through hidden messages in Led Zeppelin's fourth album, but I kept that to myself.

"Why'd the Addamses *really* sell Shangri-La?" I asked, thinking I already knew the answer.

"The thievery got to be too much. The police were brought in, but of course no one ever found anything. Mrs. Krupps was hiding the stolen loot right under everyone's noses and never had to transport any of it. People got to talking about the place being haunted. The Addamses grew frustrated and pulled up roots. They built elsewhere. Somewhere on the upper Mississippi, if memory serves."

"And the stolen jewelry?"

"Never found."

"Think she took it with her back to New York?"

He rubbed his cheek. "The police were pretty thick around Battle Lake at the end. A smart woman would have hidden the jewelry and come back later for it."

My thoughts exactly. And all the evidence I had so far indicated that Mrs. Regina Krupps had been very smart and for some reason *hadn't* returned for her jewelry.

The treasure was still in Battle Lake.

I couldn't wait to find out if Ron had broken the code.

Chapter 24

The Battle Lake Police Department was on my way back to the library, and I ducked in. This was the second time in two months that I'd voluntarily visited the PD, which was a record for a small-town girl. When you grew up in an area where violent crime consisted of cow tipping, and "vandalism" was just a fancy word for toilet-papering a house, you got used to cops being more of an obstacle to a good buzz than a real necessity.

Gary Wohnt sat at his desk in the front room. Actually, his desk *was* the front room, with a handful of chairs and filing cabinets thrown around to distract from the faux-wood paneling. He glanced up when I entered, then looked right back down.

"Hello, Chief Wohnt."

"I suppose you found another body." He stated this as fact, as if it were the natural order of things.

"Nope." I was determined to remain perky. "No body. *Nobody.* Ha!"

Gary was immune to perkiness. He pulled out a pot of lip balm from his chest pocket and slathered it on his lips. Clearly, he'd been trained in the art of mind games and was trying to get me to blurt out a confession for some unnamed crime by creating an uncomfortable silence. I needed to stay focused.

"Anyhow, Chief. You know that guy who was shot at Shangri-La last night?"

Silence.

"By the ringmaster from the Romanov Traveling Theater group?"

He pulled out a pack of Big League Chew and stuffed the pink shreds into his cheek. I caught a whiff and was reminded of simpler days, when the big excitement in my life had been staying up to watch Mutual of Omaha's *Wild Kingdom*. Would Jim get impaled by the waterbuck or have a goofy run-in with the vervet monkey? Tune in next week.

"Look, you know who I'm talking about." My patience was running thin. "The guy who was killed by the ringmaster at Shangri-La last night. I have a right to this information as a citizen and reporter." I hoped this was true.

"He wasn't killed."

"Thank you. Where can I find him?"

The chief leaned back in his chair and switched his gum wad to the other cheek. "When you find out, you tell me."

"What?"

"He was transported to Lake Region Hospital last night. Somewhere between the ambulance and the hospital room, he disappeared. We have an APB out for him and the shooter."

"You what? You lost a gunshot victim?" I was having a hard time conceiving of a cock-up on this level. "What about the Romanov troupe?"

"Left town."

"I can understand losing one actor, but a whole theater company?"

He blinked quietly at me—*blink blink*—before returning to his paperwork.

"You know," I said, annoyed, "maybe you should spend less people power on raiding fields and more on not losing shooters and their victims."

No reply.

"Say, speaking of field drinking, is it true that it's down 43 percent in the Battle Lake area?"

"Yup."

"Thanks." I left more frazzled than when I'd arrived, but at least I'd fact-checked the press release.

As I walked down the street, the information of the past three days swirled in my head like floaters in the toilet. Shirly'd confirmed that Regina Krupps had been stealing jewelry back in the twenties. He also said her husband disappeared during the same period, and that the Addamses never knew about the moonshining operation.

Fast-forward to today.

All the anecdotal evidence I'd accumulated indicated that Regina hid her stolen booty at Shangri-La and never returned for it, and that she'd confided in Samantha, who then told Jason, where to look.

At the same time they were looking for the stolen jewelry, the *Pioneer Press* ran a connected contest. Next, a fake dead body was planted in the lake near Shangri-La. Finally, a man was shot by his theatrical boss, and then he and the boss disappeared before anyone could question them.

I wasn't a big believer in coincidences, and they were piling up.

I headed to the *Recall* office to check on Ron's decoding. He was on the phone, a string of cherry licorice in his mouth and his wife on his lap. She wore a Walkman and was writhing and humming.

I tried waiting until either the phone call or his wife finished, but both looked committed to the long haul. "Ron," I hissed.

He waved dismissively in my direction.

"Ron! Did you finish that thing I left?"

He glared. "I'm on the phone!"

"Okay, I'll go. Just tell me if you finished that puzzle."

He made another shooing motion and took a big bite of licorice. His wife bent over and took a slow bite off the other end, more tramp than lady. Nothing was worth this. I turned to go.

"Wait!" Ron slapped his hand over the mouthpiece and handed the rest of the licorice to his wife. "That performer who was shot last night called, said he had a story to tell. I said to ring you at the library since you were writing the article." His eyebrows met over his nose. "Why aren't you at the library?"

I threw up my hands in exasperation. "Because I'm trying to write all the stupid stories you've assigned me!"

Ron didn't hear me. He'd already returned his attention to the call. I raced to the library. The circus performer's story could be the break I was waiting for to get Jason in real trouble. I just hoped I hadn't missed the phone call.

When I barreled into the library, I found it empty except for the books and Mrs. Berns soul-kissing the middle-aged, unmarried owner of Trim and Tan. "Mrs. Berns! Did anyone call while I was out?"

She was oblivious to the outside world, but Dave jumped away, his cheeks pink. He tried to make like I'd just caught them in the middle of a conversation. "Sure, sign me up for the library newsletter. And you have my name and address right down there. Very good. Good. Okay then, bye!" He stumbled out the door, tripping over his own feet.

Mrs. Berns wiped her mouth and smiled at his retreating figure. "He'll be back."

"Did anyone call for me?"

"A few people. You know, you're a very popular girl." She doddered toward the door, her purse in hand. "I left the keys on the counter."

"Wait. Did they say who they were?"

She fluffed her apricot hair and pursed her lips. "I'm sure they did. It would be rude not to." She continued toward the exit.

I tried to keep my voice level. "Who called for me, and what did they have to say?"

She sighed in a put-upon way. "A Wicket W. Warrick called. Said you'd want to talk to him because he had a good story. He said he'd call back tomorrow about the same time, and if you weren't here, you'd be shit outta luck. I didn't care for him one bit. That's no way to talk to a lady."

Warrick must have been the gunshot victim who'd disappeared. "Who else called?"

"Gina, that nice girl married to that good-for-nothing Hokum boy. She said she'd talk to you tonight. And I think that was it."

"Thank you." My shoulders unclenched. "I appreciate you opening up the library for me. That was really nice."

"That's a ten-four, good buddy." Mrs. Berns set off the book alarms as she passed through them, but I didn't stop her. I figured a few paperbacks were a fair trade for helping a friend out of a jam.

I sat down heavily in my front-desk chair. Until Ron broke the code or Wicket W. Warrick called to let me know why he'd been shot and then disappeared, there was nothing to do but wait.

The thing was, I was a terrible waiter, and I was too antsy to do anything productive, which left me in mental purgatory. I started doodling on the scrap paper at the front desk, using one of the standard-issue library mini-pencils. I began with a rainbow and clouds and then sketched a cool lake beneath, one full of one-dimensional fish smiling at each other. Two fish seemed to be of the same genus, so I drew a little hat and tuxedo on one and a wedding dress on the other. I added a clam to officiate and drew a large heart around the love trio.

The drawing irritated an itch from my last interview with Shirly. What had happened to Bradford Krupps, husband to Regina? Her obituary said he'd preceded her in death, but Shirly made it sound like he'd fallen off the face of the earth. I went back online to the *Niagara Gazette* website where I'd found Regina's obituary.

The newspaper listed their contact information, so I called and asked if they had any more insight into the Krupps family besides what was listed in the recent obituary. The woman on the other end was friendly but otherwise not helpful. "Regina Krupps was well known in the area, but I don't remember a husband. You say he was mentioned in the obituary?"

"Yes. It says he preceded her in death. I'm doing a local article on her philanthropy, and I wanted to know how involved he was."

"Well, I'll need to have someone call you back. Could you spell your name for me, please?"

I dreaded spelling my name over the phone. I had a disturbing disorder where I was hellishly tempted to utter vulgar matches for the letters—*M* as in "muffin top," *I* as in "intercourse," et cetera. I was thinking of doing some volunteer work so if I ever surrendered to the compulsion, I'd have a karmic buffer. "Mira James, just like it sounds. Thank you so much for your time!"

"Not a problem. You should get a callback soon."

Which left me with more waiting. Might as well hop online to search for a dessert recipe for my *Recall* column. There was a suggestions envelope taped on my desk, but the only recipes I found in there demanded cream of mushroom soup (even the desserts), and I wasn't going to stoop that low.

Besides, the internet had so far provided great ideas. Case in point: the current search had just turned up something called "Snowman's Balls" and another dessert named "Barbecued Spiced Bananas." The first required two cups of ground graham crackers, one cup of powdered sugar, two tablespoons cocoa, one cup of chopped nuts, a quarter cup coconut syrup, a quarter cup brandy, and shredded coconut. You stuck it all in a bowl except for the coconut, mixed it, and rolled it in the coconut shreds.

Voila! Snowman's balls.

It was out of season, though, and not as easy to make as the spiced bananas, offered to me courtesy of the website Sancho's Disturbing Recipes of the Eerie Past. Barbecuing bananas required a hand of bananas peeled and placed on double-thickness, heavy-duty aluminum foil. Brush them with lemon juice, sprinkle generously with brown sugar, dust with cinnamon or nutmeg, and dot with butter. Finally, pucker the tinfoil tightly around this tropical surprise and place it on the grill for seven to eight minutes.

It sounded delicious and looked completely phallic, especially, I imagined, when served with hot dogs, as the website suggested. There was nothing to inspire dinnertime conversation like a whole plateful of penis-shaped food. Maybe next week I'd pay homage to a different body part in my recipe column.

Recipe downloaded and emailed to Ron, I dusted and tried to keep my mind busy. Fortunately, the library crowd began to pick up. I caught snatches of conversation, most of them about the *Pioneer Press* contest. Apparently, a team of professional divers was camping at Glendalough State Park, and someone had heard Channel 5 KSAX out of Alexandria was going to run a story about the contest on tonight's newscast.

I'd given up on finding the planted box as soon as I realized the real diamonds were still around. Having a redneck poop in my tub had also reprioritized my life. Still, it was kind of exciting to think that someone might find a box worth $5,000.

I was surprised to discover I was feeling slightly territorial. I wanted a local to find the box, and I wanted the town to put on a nice face for the world. There really were a lot of good people living in Battle Lake. I didn't want strangers making fun of them.

That was my job.

Sal Heike appeared at my desk holding two books, one on organic gardening and the other on filing for bankruptcy. I was about to check her out when the phone rang. I excused myself to answer it.

"Is this Mira James?"

"Yes, it is. What can I do for you?"

"Hi! I'm Elizabeth Tang with the *Niagara Gazette*. Our receptionist told me you called earlier looking for information on Bradford Krupps."

Chapter 25

My pulse picked up.

"Thanks for returning my call!" I hurried to recall the lie I'd told the receptionist. "I'm writing an article on the Krupps family's history here in Minnesota. I have most of the info I need, but there's one discrepancy. My sources indicate Mr. Krupps disappeared sometime in the 1920s. The obituary you folks ran three weeks ago said he died. Do you know which it is?"

"Probably both." The sound of paper swishing came down through the line. "I dug up what we have on them after I received your message. There isn't much, but we do have an article that ran when the Niagara County Center for the Arts was built in 1940. Although Mr. Krupps is named as a contributor for the Center, the piece states, 'He was last seen in Otter Tail County, Minnesota, in the summer of 1929. Mr. Krupps is believed dead, and Mrs. Krupps dedicates this building to the loving memory of him.'"

"Wow. So he might be alive?"

"I doubt it. Mrs. Krupps was 104 when she passed last month, and her husband was older than her when they married. If he didn't die in Minnesota in the twenties, he's likely passed since of natural causes. Why the interest in him again?"

"Oh, it's not him so much." I drummed my fingers on the counter, the lie coming easily. "I want to make sure my article on Regina is accurate before I run it. I'll just mark him down as deceased."

"That's what we did in the obituary. It made the most sense." She hesitated for a moment. "That Mrs. Krupps was quite the woman. I bet you didn't have any trouble finding dirt on her!"

"You got that right!" I was bluffing, of course. "You guys have the same experiences with her out there?"

"Oh yes. She was fairly high profile because of all the money she came into when she married Bradford Krupps. It was a classic rags-to-riches story. Too bad she was crazy."

"You got that right! Kooky Krupps, that's how they refer to her around here."

"I believe it. That lady was as loopy as the day is long. One minute she'd be at a public event as nice and normal as apple pie, and the next day she'd be calling the local radio station complaining about the government poisoning her water. I imagine a psychiatrist would have been able to diagnose her, if she'd ever gone to one."

"No doubt."

"Send me a copy of your piece when you're done. I'd be interested in reading it."

Great. Now I'd have to write a fake article. "You got it. Thank you for your time, Ms. Tang. You've been helpful!"

"Not a problem. We writers need to stick together. Let me know if I can be of any more help."

"Will do." I discarded the sourness at all the lies I'd just told and kept the warm feeling I got from being called a writer long after we hung up. Well, I planned to anyhow, until Kennie Rogers rumbled in and chilled the goodness right out of me.

I finished checking out a very patient Sal as Kennie strode to the counter, her powerful perfume preceding her like acid rain. As usual, her face was overly made up, but her hair distracted from that. She'd perched a frizzy bun made from curls two shades darker than her own hair on the crown of her head. The hairpiece reminded me of a nesting chipmunk, but maybe that was because of the lime-green Alvin and the Chipmunks beach cover-up she wore above her platform rainbow flip-flops.

"Mira James, you sure know how to pick 'em! That Jason Blunt was quite the kisser. And what in the name of Dixie happened to your head?"

I felt my forehead, worried, and rubbed across my June-bug goose egg. I had in point of fact forgotten about it, and no one else had mentioned it. "Don't forget that Jason's dangerous. Also, I ran into a bug."

She shook her head. "Well, sweetie, you don't have to tell the truth, but you can lie better than that. Now, about that job last night."

I reached for my purse.

"Not necessary." She held up a hand. "I couldn't charge you for all the fun I had at Shangri-La. I consider kissing a handsome man volunteer work to be conducted for the greater good of Kennie." She yanked icy pink lipstick out of her bag and delicately applied it to her lips and their greater surroundings. "I do have a favor I need in return, though."

My stomach tensed. Why was I thinking that it'd be a lot cheaper to pay cash?

"I need you to babysit my nephew tonight."

Whew. "I didn't know you had brothers or sisters."

She made a pout. "Okay, if you're going to play it that way. He's not my nephew, he's a friend of Gary's in town from Alaska. We're supposed to show him a good time, and I don't want to entertain the dolt all night long. It seems like a fair trade, considering what I did for you last night. You in?"

I was so not in that it was ridiculous. "I'd love to, Kennie—really, really love to—spend the night with you, Gary Wohnt, and some strange guy from Alaska, but I have to work."

"Sweetie, where could you possibly work at night?" Her voice was peaches and cream and arsenic.

"Newspaper work."

"Give me that phone." She grabbed the handset and dialed Ron before I knew what was happening. Of course he said I didn't need to work any specific hours, as long as I got my articles in before deadline.

"We're set, darling," Kennie crowed to me. "I'll pick you up at seven. I heard at the Turtle Stew that you're staying at Gina's, right? Look pretty. Oh, and Ronnie said he won't have time to get to your puzzle code until tomorrow."

And just like that, she sashayed out the door, leaving me in her hurricane wake. I was shocked.

No, I was horrified.

A blind double date with Kennie and Gary was making a turd in the tub look like pennies from heaven. I wondered if I could get Mrs. Berns to pinch-hit for me again.

Sigh. I probably could, but Kennie had done me a favor, and I owed her one.

At least I'd have a few hours where I wouldn't have to worry about Jason assaulting me.

Chapter 26

When I returned to Gina's and told her about my "date," she laughed until she had hiccups. She even called Leif at work to share the story. I could hear him hooting over the phone from across the room. So glad my misery was bringing them closer. Gina made me swear to wake her up and tell her all about the blind date no matter how late it went.

"Oh, this won't be going late."

"Oh, I don't know," she said teasingly. "He might be your magical mystery man."

I grimaced. "I don't envision Kennie and Gary being the garnish on my plate of love. In fact, I need to get myself repulsive and quick to keep this short and sweet. Or just short and short."

"Want me to curl your hair?" Her eyes sparkled with mischief.

"No." The day's ponytail would do just fine. "There's not time. It's an early dinner."

"Want to borrow my blue eye shadow?"

"No." Tiger Pop and Luna were giving me weird looks. They sensed I shouldn't go on this date.

"Can I come spy on you?"

"No."

She sighed. "Well, then I'll just ding around my house until you get home."

"Great."

She plopped next to me on the couch facing the picture window. We waited in relative silence punctuated by her sporadic bursts of giggling. I found small comfort in the fact that my misery was distracting her from hers.

I was almost relieved when Kennie pulled up in her trademark pink two-door 1967 Plymouth Barracuda fastback with a V-8 and roaring glass packs (in case anyone wasn't paying attention). Getting tonight done and over with was preferable to waiting for it to happen because there was no way anything could be as bad as I was imagining.

"Yoo-hoo!" Kennie waved out the car window and honked.

Gina dragged me off the couch and shoved me out the door, giving my butt a good pinch. Halfway to the car, the passenger-side door opened and Gary Wohnt stepped out, turning immediately to pull his seat forward. Another head popped out, this one gray and moist-looking. As my date stood, I guessed he was about five foot ten, maybe fifteen years older than me, with a broad, pork-white face accented by large, square glasses. He was stout but not overweight and wore a yellowed tank top and shorts. Except for his jowls, he was unremarkable.

Maybe this wouldn't be heinous.

At least he appeared to have all his teeth.

That's when his hand appeared from behind his back, revealing a wrist corsage laid out in a plastic take-out box like a body in a coffin. Gina slammed the house door shut behind me, but I could hear her cackling through the wood, followed by a crash like she'd fallen over in a fit of giggles.

"Hello, little lady," he said, as we met on the sidewalk. "I'm Ody."

"Hi, Ody." I gestured at the pink and blue flower mound. "Is that for me?"

"I don't see any other pretty girls around here." He slipped the carnations out of the plastic to-go case, stretched the elastic band, and offered it up. "May I?"

I let him slide it on. What did I have to prove? As long as it didn't house a tracking device that would prevent me from being able to escape later, I was good. "Thanks, Ody."

"Thank you for—"

Kennie laid on her horn. "Save it for when she's drunk, Ody. I'm hungry!"

I crawled in behind Kennie's seat. Ody landed next to me, drowning us both in the chemical-sweet smell of Old Spice. "Where're we going?" I asked Kennie.

"Halverson Park for a picnic. Gary thought it would be romantic." Kennie squeezed his knee at the same time I squeezed my throat to keep the bile down.

I made a stab at friendliness. "So, Chief Wohnt, since you're off duty, can I call you Gary?"

He glared holes through the windshield. He wasn't returning Kennie's affection, either. The two of them never acted like they were dating when they were in public, though the whole town assumed they were a couple. I wondered if Chief Wohnt would let his guard down tonight.

And speaking of chiefs, I was happy to be spending the first part of the night at the feet of Chief Wenonga, my favorite twenty-three-foot-tall fiberglass Indian. The effigy had been erected at Halverson Park in 1979 as a way to "honor" the Ojibwe, the original settlers of Battle Lake. The real Chief Wenonga had lived over a hundred and fifty years ago. The fiberglass rendition of him was a tall woman's wet dream. He was dark and steely-eyed in an alpha-male kind of way, with a washboard stomach and a nice package.

I'd been having adult dreams starring Chief Wenonga for a few weeks now. Freud would likely attribute this attraction to unattainable fiberglass men to having lost my father in my teens, but for me, it was all about hope. Some people longed for Brad Pitt. I had Chief Wenonga. It was only crazy if you told someone else.

Ody hadn't said two words since Kennie scolded him outside Gina's, and that was fine by me. Kennie parked the car in the Halverson lot, and we all filed to the lone picnic table near Chief Wenonga's base. I winked up at him. He pretended he didn't see me. It was our game.

"Hope you like smoked fish!" Ody smiled and straddled a bench as Kennie unloaded the picnic basket. "Brought it all the way from Alaska!"

I liked smoked fish about as well as I liked smoked toes, but I could do the small-talk game. I was actually a little curious about what sort of person would be friends with Gary Wohnt. "What kind of work do you do in Alaska?"

Ody's pale face grew serious. "I'm a peace officer, just like my good friend and fellow rascal Gary Wohnt. God's work in God's country."

"How about for fun?" I asked.

"That's where it gets interesting." He shifted his weight so he could lean toward me, his hands up like the goalposts on a football field. "I'm one of those guys who likes to live for the moment, see?"

"Sure."

"Yeah. Some people say, 'This is my life. What am I going to do with it?' I say, 'This is fishing season. What kind of bait do I need?'" Ody laughed, and Gary nodded approvingly.

I felt empty as a pocket. These were not my people.

"I have to pee." I rose and walked over to the public bathrooms, wondering if I could "accidentally" trip and break my itchy wrist corsage. My cutoffs and white T-shirt simply did not do it justice. Inside the bathroom stall, I dropped my bottoms and balanced over the toilet seat perched on top of a hole in the ground. The salty, pungent odor of outhouse and darkness closed in on me, and I held the carnations close to my nose to cover the smell.

I peed, listening to the tinkling echo in the pit. I dreamed of having to throw up so I could stay in the outhouse longer. Straight across from me, someone had scrawled, *I screwed your mother!* Down and to the left, someone else had written, *Go home dad. You're drunk!* I did a little more recreational reading until my legs started quivering.

I finished my business and reluctantly left the stall, heading to the wall mirror. It was wavy and hand-pounded, like polished steel, and I couldn't see myself very well because the only light trickled through a square opening near the ceiling. I squirted out some hand sanitizer from the dispenser and decided I couldn't hide any longer.

On my way out, I passed a large scrawl that read, *No matter how good she looks, some other guy is sick and tired of putting up with her crap.* I crossed it out with a pen tied to the wall next to the cleaning schedule and wrote, *I think, therefore I am single.* Not one of my wittier moments, but at least I'd made a mark.

I'd always wondered who had the energy to write on bathroom walls. Now I knew. It was folks on blind dates. I steeled myself and stepped out into the lowering sun. Where I stood now, with Chief Wenonga and the terrible trio behind me, I could see the full brilliance of West Battle Lake. The sun was on the far side, sliding into the lavender pillow of the horizon, and sailboats and fishing boats glided across the lake. The faraway sounds of kids swimming and splashing echoed across the water.

A light breeze kept the buzzing mosquitoes to a minimum, and the temperature was still in the eighties but dropping. It would be a beautiful night. I was going to go back to the picnic table, eat my food, make polite small talk, and walk back to Gina's. This wasn't so bad. I could do this.

"Hey, Mira," Kennie called, waving her jangly-braceleted arm. "Come over here and tell us if this looks infected to you!"

Curse words.

Chapter 27

I shuffled over and dutifully examined the scabby wound on Ody's knee. When I told him I thought salve and a Band-Aid would take care of it, he looked relieved and adjusted his glasses. "I had a partner who lost part of a leg to a scratch gone bad. Right below his knee. I swore that was never going to happen to me."

"It's good to have dreams, Ody." If there were such a thing as date indemnity, I would be considered uninsurable. The thing was, at least with Ody, I was pretty sure I knew what I was getting.

The four of us sat down to a meal of smoked salmon (which looked raw and tasted like a salty washrag doused in lighter fluid), Easy Cheese, crackers, and Boone's Farm strawberry wine. ("It's not Boone's *Farm*, honey, it's *Boone's* Farm," Kennie had corrected me as she poured it.)

For dessert, we ate Oreos, which so far was the high point of the evening. Fortunately, no one talked as we ate. Once the cheese can was empty and the fish was a grease-slick memory, the men sat back and began sucking leftovers out of their teeth.

Ody undid the top button of his Wrangler shorts to get a little more breathing room. "I caught, cleaned, and smoked that salmon myself, Mira," he said. "I'm real good with fish."

Maybe the Boone's Farm was getting to me, but I could have sworn that was some sort of lewd remark. "I don't like fishing, and I don't really like fish, to tell you the truth. They're too wet. I like dry food." I rubbed at my forehead, trying to fend off a headache. "Tater Tots and scones, that sort of thing."

This sparked some indignation in Ody, who launched into a lecture about the benefits of eating God's creatures fresh from their habitat. I tuned him out and looked around for an escape. I spotted it in the form of Jed strolling down the road past the park. He must have been walking from town back to the Last Resort.

"Hey, Jed!" I desperately waved him over before I realized he was with Johnny Leeson. I pulled my hand back like it was holding a rip cord and clamped my mouth shut. Johnny couldn't see me on this date!

But obviously this had to be the single time in his life that Jed was actually paying attention. He loped over and Johnny followed, doing his casual Adonis thing. I wished desperately to disappear.

"Hey, Mira," Jed said. "You on a double date?"

He wore a Def Leppard T-shirt over torn jeans, and a red bandanna held back his brown curls. Johnny had on a bright white T-shirt, which matched his smile and set off his nut-brown skin. The shirt hugged his broad shoulders and just skimmed the second snap of his button-fly Levi's, nicely showcasing his narrow hips. Even from here, I knew he smelled clean, like fresh laundry and newly cut grass.

Kennie, on the other hand, was still wearing her Alvin and the Chipmunks getup with her nesting hair, Gary Wohnt had pulled down his mirrored sunglasses and was reapplying lip balm, and Ody, with the top button of his Wrangler shorts undone, smelled of the fish he was still sucking from his eyeteeth.

"No, Jed," I said. "I was just visiting with these people."

Ody leaned over and brushed hair from my face. At least that's what I think he meant to do, but he misjudged the distance and bonked me in the forehead instead. "No need to be modest, girl. I ain't ashamed to be with you."

Now my *face* smelled like fish. I swallowed a hot ball of humiliation and turned to Jed, ignoring the strange and intense look Johnny was giving me. He was probably downgrading me from "dork" to "do not touch."

I tried smiling. "What are you two up to?" I asked Jed.

"We're on our way back from running some errands for my mom. We figured it'd be a waste of a good night to drive. Hey, man, that show at Shangri-La was a kicker, no? When you disappeared and all that?" He nodded agreeably.

Belatedly, I remembered that the last time I'd seen Jed was immediately after I stunned him and his bongo-playing compadre in the woods near Shangri-La. My life had been quite a ride the past few days.

Johnny had moved off and was studying Chief Wenonga, his shoulders in an angry set. Or was I imagining it? His profile was lean and muscular, and his strong hands, the ones I often imagined twisted in my hair as he pulled me in for a passionate kiss, were fisted at his sides. I returned my attention to Jed, who didn't seem bothered at all that me and Z-Force had made his hair extra curly that night. "Yeah, sorry about the stun gun. I was a little freaked out."

"What?" Jed asked.

"The shock I gave you when I jumped out of the bongo."

Jed's smile was confused but welcoming.

"You know, when I jumped out, zapped you, and you fell to the ground?"

Jed stared at Gary Wohnt and then back at me, winking conspiratorially. "Sure, you *zapped* me. I was real *zapped* that night."

Cripes. Jed didn't even know I'd stun-gunned him. He thought it was just another high. "Yeah, Jed, you sure were." I had to raise my voice to be heard over the now-frenzied tooth-sucking coming from the cop dates. I longed to tap out "Help Me" in Morse code, desperate to let Johnny know that I wasn't on a date, but the truth was, I *was* on a date, and I had no reason to think he cared. Besides, I didn't know Morse code.

I was miserable.

"Okay then, we'll see you around," Jed said, scratching his hair beneath the bandanna. "Say, Chief Wohnt, when will we get back that dive suit that Mira found in Whiskey?"

"When we find out who planted the body," he growled.

"That makes sense," he said agreeably, "but it'd sure be nice to rent it out to someone else."

I was reminded how tight money was in the Heike household. Add one more to the pile of reasons I needed to get to the bottom of this story, and quickly.

Jed and Johnny took off, Johnny flashing me one last inscrutable glance. I was left alone to make conversation in the wasteland. I examined my three options—Kennie, who was filing her nails; Ody, who was picking at his scab; and Gary Wohnt.

"So, Chief, you still have the Last Resort dive suit that body was in?"

Silence.

"Did you also confiscate the suits from the other divers who rented them from the Last Resort?"

Gary shifted a toothpick from one side of his mouth to the other. I'd given up on him answering me when he finally spoke. "We investigated the people who rented them. They are all either staying at the Last Resort or at Glendalough, and they all came up clean. We did not take their dive suits."

"None of the dive suit renters were staying at Shangri-La?" I was thinking of Jason.

"None."

"Not even *one*?"

"Nope."

I shielded my eyes from the sun so I could watch Jed and Johnny walking away. Why had Jed lied to me about Jason Blunt, current Shangri-La resident extraordinaire, renting three dive suits from him? Then I remembered the water puddle under the dive suit I'd borrowed, the dive suit he claimed hadn't been used in a long time.

Maybe Jason hadn't *rented* his suits—maybe he'd borrowed them just like I had. Jed had mentioned that he'd partied with Jason. Had he done more? Was he Jason's accomplice in all this? Goofy stoner Jed? I shook my head. I refused to believe it.

My stomach was roiling, and now it wasn't just because I'd eaten canned cheese and questionable fish. "I don't feel so good. I think I need to go home."

Kennie appeared indignant. "The evening is young! I spent a lot more time working for you last night, and I didn't even get a free meal out of it."

Ody burped. "I'd walk you home, but these here legs are more ornamental than functional." He winked. Or he had something in his eye. "When will we be meeting again, little lady?"

I tried to be vague without being rude. "Oh, you'll know when we meet again." Because I'll be the one screaming and running the other way. "Thank you for the . . . food. And Kennie, I think we're even."

She scowled, but I would not be deterred. I needed self-respect and sleep. I saluted Chief Wenonga and hightailed it to Gina's couch.

Chapter 28

When I woke the next day, Gina was sitting at the foot of the sofa drinking coffee and waiting for me to open my eyes with all the patience of a kid on Christmas morning. She had already walked, fed, and watered Luna and opened a pouch of Tender Vittles for Tiger Pop. All that was left to do was try and stare me awake.

As soon as I stirred, she pounced. "Why didn't you wake me up when you got home?"

"Because I figured if you were asleep by nine, you probably needed to stay asleep." I stretched and tugged the sheet over my head. I hated sleeping over at other people's houses. It wasn't comfortable.

"You were home by nine? No kissing?"

"No kissing. I did get to see the lower end of his belly button when he unsnapped his pants so he could eat more, though."

"You're pulling my leg." Her voice was drenched in disbelief. "I wipe other people's butts for a living, and that grosses me right out."

I pulled the sheet down and squinted at her. "Yeah. The best part came when Johnny Leeson met my date."

She slammed her coffee down and covered her mouth with both hands. "NO! Hot Johnny saw you on a date with a greasy old cop?"

"Ody was his name."

"Girl, you lost some points there."

"You think?"

Gina frowned. "Your timing's not great. Word on the street is Johnny just broke up with Liza. Last night would have been a good time to appear available."

I groaned and replayed the strange looks Johnny had given me. If he'd had any thoughts of auditioning me for Liza's replacement, the secondhand Ody all over me would've killed that.

Gina studied my face and laughed kindly. "It's not that bad. We've all been on crappy dates, even Johnny. Anyhow, I gotta go to work. What's on your plate for today?"

"I'm not sure yet. How well do you know Jed Heike?" I shared how he'd misled me about renting dive suits to Jason and how I was nursing a bad feeling that he was somehow connected to the planted dead body and wounded circus performer.

Gina screwed up her face, considering. "You know, I did hear that the Last Resort was going under. They don't get enough business. You think he'd hook up with Jason for the money?"

"I think he'd do anything to help out his parents."

Gina frowned. "Even steal?"

I rubbed my face, smelling the odor of last night's salmon even though I'd showered before bed. "I don't want to believe it, but you've got to admit his lying is suspicious."

She crossed her arms. "All I'm saying is you don't want to spend the energy worrying about what Jed is up to until you find out what's *really* going on."

"Fair." I looked over at the clock. "Aren't you late for work?"

"I don't start until eight today. The bathroom is all yours." Gina shuffled off into the kitchen and then turned back to me with a girlish smile. "Leif and I are going out on Friday. He said it's going to be a surprise, but I hope he takes me to the casino."

I mirrored her smile. "That's great, G. And you guys have set up counseling appointments?"

She stared at her feet. "We might. Right now we just want to try it the old-fashioned way."

Around here, and maybe everywhere in the world, "the old-fashioned way" meant he did what he wanted and she told herself it was her job to love him, not change him. It made me too sad to comment, so I just nodded.

I cleaned myself up, gave Luna and Tiger Pop some attention, and was in the library by nine. I used the time before opening to tend to the duties I'd been neglecting the last few days. I shelved books, vacuumed, watered plants, even cleaned the windows. I also responded to a handful of email questions and organized the library mail, which was mainly book catalogs and overdue fines getting paid.

When the call came, I was basking in the afterglow of a vigorous organizing session, my face flushed and wearing a rare relaxed smile.

"Yeah, this the newspaper lady?" The voice on the other end of the line was distinctly male, but high, like it was piped through a flute.

"I'm a reporter at the *Battle Lake Recall*." My heartbeat did a little dance. "Are you the guy who was shot Monday night?"

I heard him puff up proudly on the other end. "That I am. Nikolai Romanov is the name, and crowd-pleasing is my game."

"Romanov? I thought your name was Wicket W. Warrick." I grabbed a miniature pencil and a sheet of paper from the printer to take notes.

He chuckled condescendingly. "That's just one of my many stage names. I didn't know who I was talking to yesterday when I called. The nature of my work requires me to cultivate an air of mystery."

"I'm sure." I sketched a pair of wide eyes. "So the Romanov Traveling Theater troupe is yours?"

"It is."

I thought back to the message he'd given Ron and then Mrs. Berns. "And you have a story to tell?"

"I do. I will relay it to you on the south shore of Whiskey Lake at midnight tonight."

"What?" I squeaked. If you look up "moron" in the dictionary, you'd find "person who meets an unfamiliar carnival performer on the lam in a secluded area at midnight."

I hedged. "How about we rendezvous when it's light out?"

"How about I tell my story to the *Pioneer Press*?"

How about I didn't give a crap about the competition. I *did* need to find out how Jason was caught up in all this, though, so I could feel safe in my home once again. I peeked into the purse I'd started carrying and reassured myself that my trusty Z-Force was still nestled inside. "Fine. Give it to me in little-kid directions."

"You know where the public-access boat landing is on Whiskey?"

"Yup."

"Go to the landing. Face the water. Walk a hundred yards to your right. I'll be waiting. Be quiet, dress in black, bring a small tape recorder, and don't be late." His voice dropped. "And come alone, or I'll disappear like dust in the wind."

Good lord. What sort of self-respecting circus performer quoted Kansas lyrics? "Fine."

I hung up and unlocked the door to let in the ten or so people who were lining up. I didn't think the library had ever been this busy. They looked like more newcomers here for the *Pioneer Press* contest. Most of them turned out to be magazine readers, which was the library equivalent of window shoppers, but a few signed up for library cards and mentioned that they were enjoying their stay.

Over lunch, I closed down for a quick dash to the Fortune Café. Nancy was behind the counter in a green-checkered apron that read, "I'm Not Gay, But My Girlfriend Is." Their sexual orientation served as a great social filter. Small-minded people avoided the café, which worked well for the rest of us. I was still surprised they hadn't been stoned right out of town, which likely made *me* the small-minded one.

Actually, the Fortune's biggest customer base was Sid and Nancy's church group. The two were active at Nordland Lutheran and were a particular favorite when it came time for the annual bake sale.

Nancy waved me to the front of the line because she knew I was on my lunch break. "What're you in the mood for today?"

"Just a garlic bagel and some jasmine tea, Nance." I slid my travel mug over to her. "Thanks."

"Say," she called over her shoulder as she worked. "Did Sid get a hold of you?"

I grabbed the tea and a napkin and angled the bagel out of her hands—she knew I didn't want a bag—and handed her my money. "No. About what?"

"I'll let her tell you. She's in back loading the oven." Nancy jerked her head toward the kitchen, wiped her hands on a towel, and turned to the customer behind me.

I felt like a trespasser when I stepped into the heart of the bakery. I'd never been back here before, and it smelled like heaven. A large oven dominated one wall, and the middle was packed with flour-dusted tables covered with rising bread and pastries in various stages of cooling, being frosted, and being filled. Off to the side was a storage room with ingredients cleanly labeled, covered, and stored on metal wire shelves. The only thing missing was Sid.

"Hello?"

"Hey, Mira!" She appeared from the back of the storage room. She was smiling, but she looked harried. She had a swipe of flour across her cheek, and her arms were loaded with trays of raw cookie-dough balls.

"Nancy said you wanted to talk to me?"

"Yeah, it's nothing really. It might just be a rumor. The divers camping out at Glendalough? Well, they were in for coffee this morning, and they said they've scoured Whiskey Lake from top to bottom, north to south, and there's no necklace in a box. Like anywhere. They were going to dive one more time, and if they didn't find anything, they planned to lodge a complaint."

My chin drew back. "So they think it was never sunk in the lake?"

"That, or someone found it and doesn't want anyone to know for some godforsaken reason. Just thought I'd pass it on, since you're the reporter and all." She loaded her cookie sheets into the oven.

"Thanks, Sid."

I didn't know what to make of this new information. Certainly, diving was not an exact science. Visibility was often poor, and objects in lakes, especially spring-fed lakes, had a tendency to shift. But the people at the *Pioneer Press* must have known this, and since they wanted the box found, if it *was* still there, it was surprising that no one had come across it yet. After all, it had been three days since the box had supposedly been hidden.

I pondered this as I walked to the *Recall* office eating my bagel. Ron was seated at the front counter when I strolled in, the phone still growing out of his ear. I waited impatiently, but he wasn't off by the time I'd finished my lunch.

So I pulled up a chair right next to him and stared at him, inches from his face.

He shooed me like a fly, but I didn't move. He finally sighed and stood up to paw through a file cabinet, the phone cradled between his shoulder and ear.

Then he passed me the pink note onto which I'd transcribed the code.

Chapter 29

I eagerly grabbed the pink paper. Ron had crossed out the letters and written new ones above, sometimes crossing out his guesses and writing on top of that. The letters were four high in some cases, but if I followed the hills, this was what the code I'd stolen from the rum room said:

With your back to the kissing tree walk seven steps northwest kneel 23 left 12 right 11 left.

There were question marks next to all three numbers, but that wasn't the beginning of my questions. What was a kissing tree? Was I supposed to kneel twenty-three times, or were there twenty-three of something remaining? Twenty-three remaining minus twelve that were right did leave eleven, but what did that mean?

This was a puzzle within a puzzle.

I yanked the list of Shangri-La's stolen jewelry out of my purse. Twenty-eight pieces were recorded missing, not including "assorted diamond earrings." That didn't seem to be what the code numbers were referring to. They almost sounded like a dance—kneel, go twenty-three steps to the left, twelve to the right, and eleven to the left. That felt a little over the top, but not surprising from a woman who'd write a secret cipher in the first place. Once I figured out what the kissing tree was, maybe this would be a lot clearer.

I dashed back to the library and searched through the Otter Tail County reference books. No mention of a kissing tree. When I went online, all I found were obscure references to musical bands and some strange religion, and even a funny website where a woman had created a virtual tree consisting of pictures of people who'd kissed her—but no Otter Tail County landmarks.

On a whim, I called over to the Senior Sunset and asked for Mrs. Berns. If there was anyone in this town who would know where people went to kiss in the 1920s, it was her.

"Yello."

"Mrs. Berns?"

"Last time I checked."

"This is Mira from over at the library. Say, do you know if there is a kissing tree in Battle Lake?"

"Oh honey, who told you that you have to be under a tree to kiss? That's malarkey. You kiss anywhere you feel like kissing!"

I could sense her getting worked up on the other end. Kissing discrimination was clearly an important issue to her. "Thanks. I'll take that to heart. But I'm writing an article on the history of love in Battle Lake, and I'm wondering if you'd heard about a place people went to make out back in the 1920s."

"Before my time," she said. "Hold on while I ask around."

Twelve minutes later, she was back on the phone, cackling. "You still here?"

"Yup." I had been paging through *Us* magazine, reading a strangely compelling article about Paris Hilton, the Zsa Zsa Gabor of the new millennium. I figured Mrs. Berns would remember me eventually.

"I forgot we were talking on the phone." I heard some more chittering in the background. "The good news is, I found out about your kissing tree. You know where Chief Wenonga sits?"

Boy, did I. And I knew where I wished he'd sit, too: right in my front yard so I could wake up to him every morning. "Yes, ma'am."

"Well, straight across the road from him, there's a little dip as you go down toward the lake. There's a grove of trees in that valley, and I guess all the kids used to sneak there to make out."

I knew the grove, and I bet it was twenty-three strides from the Chief, give or take. That might account for one number, only the Chief was built fifty years after Regina would have hidden the jewels.

The only thing for it was to check out the area after I closed the library.

Chapter 30

The afternoon dragged on like yet another war documentary on the History Channel, but closing time finally arrived. Normally, I'd let people finish what they were doing before I locked up, but that afternoon I physically herded people out of the library. Just as I was guiding the last person out of the foyer, Leylanda tried to sneak in with Peyton for some last-minute reading.

I was having none of it.

"We just need a few books," Leylanda said, appearing more uptight than usual.

"It's five after. It's past closing time. Come back tomorrow."

Peyton wiped at her nose, her pigtails pointing straight out of each side of her head. "Mom wants to make carob cookies tonight," she said, her eyes sad. "It was my idea to get a book instead."

My own mother had gone through a health food phase, which was how I knew that carob was actually toe jam masquerading as a chocolate replacement. "Okay, sweetie. You go grab what you want, and your mom and I'll wait here. You don't even have to check it out."

I wasn't letting Leylanda past the foyer. She'd make herself at home just to annoy me. She glared at me, crossing her arms and sticking out her chin. But the silence grew to be too much for her, and she started to make conversation against her will.

"You were talking with Jason Blunt yesterday near the turtle races," she said.

"Sure. *Talking*." She must have seen him push me down.

She made a humming noise. "He's quite a man."

"If by that you mean he's an abusive dink, then I agree completely." Peyton was grabbing three of the most colorful new arrivals across the room. I turned to Leylanda. "How do you know him, anyhow? He doesn't seem like your type."

She sniffed. "We went to high school together. As to my type, you probably don't understand the nature of testosterone. You see, I am an alpha female, and I require an alpha male." She spoke with the certainty of someone who'd read a lot of articles on the subject.

Despite how much she annoyed me, my heart went out to her. She was in the early stages of making a terrible but common error—mistaking one-way attention for a two-way attraction. And while I was no fan of hers, I adored Peyton.

"Leylanda," I said, "you've got a wonderful kid, and I'm sure you've got some good qualities, if you relaxed a little. So don't be sucked in by Jason's nice-guy front. He's an insecure, violent creep." I saved my big gun for last, leaning in so she'd get the full impact. "And he doesn't recycle."

I had no idea if this was true, but it got the reaction I was after. Leylanda sucked in her breath, her eyes wide. "Come on, Peyton!" she said without taking her gaze off me. "Mommy says it's time to go! Come on now!"

Peyton ran across the room to show me the books she'd selected, her pigtails waving and a triumphant look on her face: *Princess Smartypants*, *Dear Girl*, and *Good Night Stories for Rebel Girls*. Man, I loved that kid. I grabbed the books and fed them to her behind the alarm sensors so she wouldn't trigger the system. She was almost through the door when she pulled free from her mom's grasp long enough to run back and hand me a stack of paper she'd been crumpling in her seven-year-old fist. I unfolded them enough to see that they were crayon drawings.

She was in the pastel stage of her artistry. The first picture featured a baby-blue house with a round yellow sun overhead, and she'd scrawled her name on the bottom in tilting green. The second picture was of an animal, but I don't think anyone short of Dr. Moreau could have identified it. The third looked like a drawing of a family sitting around a dinner table. At the bottom, she'd spelled out "math lab" in sweet, crooked letters.

Of course that's what Leylanda calls homework time, I thought, as I locked the library behind me. I was hurrying toward Chief Wenonga, walking fast but also fumbling to tuck the drawings into my purse.

That was my excuse for smacking straight into Johnny Leeson, knocking both of us on our bumpers.

Chapter 31

I popped up first, dancing around like a fighter before a match. "Sorry, Johnny! I didn't see you!" I held out my hand.

He grabbed it and pulled himself up.

"You okay?" I asked.

"Yeah, I'm fine." He brushed dirt off his jeans, and I spotted a raw spot on his palm.

"Shoot, I'm sorry. Look." I reached out for him and then jerked back. "You scraped your hand."

He rubbed it on his pants. "It's not a big deal, Mira. It's just a scrape. I'll be fine." He did an unconscious head toss that moved his golden hair out of his eyes.

I tried to steady my heartbeat. I was suddenly self-conscious of the green-and-yellow bump pushing out of my noggin like a horn. He must have seen it last night, but there'd been too many other horrors happening for me to worry about my appearance. I moved my hand toward my forehead, letting it float there. "Nice night, huh?"

He glanced around, weighing the accuracy of my comment. "It is. How're your tomatoes holding up? Is the dill keeping the bugs away?"

"Yeah, but I think I'm overwatering. The color on the tomato leaves isn't so good." My hand was still perched in front of my lump. I drummed the side of my head in what I hoped was a nonchalant gesture.

He nodded, a reluctant smile teasing the corners of his mouth. "That can happen. We have some automatic tomato waterers at the nursery so you don't have that problem. Stop by and I'll show 'em to you."

"That would be great!" I was smiling right up until the finch flew into the side of my skull, right behind the hand I was holding up, and dropped to the pavement, stunned. I shrieked and jumped back. It shook its feathery little head, pooped, and took off again.

"Ack!" I yelled.

Johnny reached toward me with his strong, tanned hands. "Are you okay? That had to hurt."

I was already hustling in the other direction, away from Johnny so he couldn't see the involuntary water filling my eyes. It wasn't even that the side of my head was throbbing, though it was. No, the most urgent problem was that the birds were finally organizing their attack, and I wasn't going to take Johnny down with me.

"Oh no, didn't hurt at all," I hollered over my shoulder, ignoring his bemused expression. "I do that all the time at home!"

I do that all the time at home? Headbutt birds??

But I had to keep moving.

It took me ten minutes to reach Halverson Park and Chief Wenonga's statue. I didn't spot any bird gangs flashing their blades on the way, so I calmed down a hair, though I had the mother of all headaches. I decided the finch had been a lone gunman, trying to protect Johnny from me, the un–Snow White.

Oh well. I was better off single.

The grove Mrs. Berns had described as Battle Lake's 1920s makeout spot was an unassuming cluster of poplars hugging the lake, with a road on one side and the Sandy Beach Resort on the other. Peonies bloomed crazily around the Sandy Beach cabins, scenting the air like white trash roses.

I pulled out Ron's notes and read "23 left, 12 right, 11 left."

I couldn't see what I had to lose. With my back to the grove, I paced twenty-three steps forward, keeping the sun on my left. Then I walked twelve steps to the right, toward Sandy Beach, which led me straight into the volleyball pit. Eleven steps in any direction still left me in the pit. Anything hidden here would have been unearthed when the resort was built, so unless Regina had buried the loot in the lake itself, I was at the wrong spot.

My stomach grew hollow, and I kicked at the court sand. Finding the jewelry before Jason would have been my trump card. My only hope now was that Nikolai Romanov would tell me something incriminating about Jason tonight.

It was a long shot.

Dejected, I headed back toward my car in the library parking lot.

I heard the siren's scream before the lights flashed into view. It was Gary Wohnt's official vehicle racing by. I had a thick, bad feeling that intensified when the squad car screeched down Oak Avenue, about seven blocks up. I started running as fast as I could. Gardening, swimming, and walking with Luna kept me in pretty good shape, but as a grownup, I hadn't found much call to run. My body didn't know what to do with itself. I made it five blocks before I was forced to slow to a brisk walk.

Oak Avenue's houses here were well-maintained ramblers situated on large wooded lots. The one exception was the freakish white box of a house where Leylanda and Peyton lived, likely all she could afford after the divorce. Chief Wohnt's car was parked in their driveway, his siren off but his lights still flashing.

The blood in my veins chilled. I'd been with Leylanda and Peyton only a half hour earlier. I could picture them tucked in the safety of their living room, reading the books Peyton had picked out, eating roasted soy nuts, and chugging organic ginger ale. I didn't want to disturb that picture, because I knew in my aching heart how quickly terrible things struck good people.

I forced my feet to move through the ominous quicksand of my fears until I reached Leylanda's front door. It was flung wide open, and inside Leylanda sat on the couch, her neighbor propping her up. Gary Wohnt knelt in front of her.

Leylanda was speaking, her voice trembling. "She wanted to read in her room alone. She wasn't out of my sight for more than ten minutes. I swear!" She was wringing her hands, and two rivers of snot ran out of her nose.

I was hit by an unbearable, aching wave of loss that I hadn't experienced as acutely since my dad died. *Peyton was missing.* I knew what it was like to be a girl alone in the world, and Peyton was too young to experience that depth of fear and loneliness. How could this have happened so soon after I was just hanging out with her?

The neighbor holding Leylanda looked up as I entered, but no one stopped me. Maybe it was because I was floating above the room, watching the actors stage their play.

Peyton. Someone had stolen her.

Chief Wohnt spoke into his shoulder radio. There was some feedback, but it crackled too much for me to make sense of it. His voice was urgent when he spoke to Leylanda. "I need to know everyone you've talked to and everywhere you've been in the last twenty-four hours."

Leylanda struggled to pull herself together, but it was beyond her. "Somebody took my daughter! She needs to sleep in her own bed or she's up all night!" Hysteria was squeezing her voice. "Who will give her the lavender sleep drops she needs?"

"You need to calm down," Wohnt urged, not unkindly. "She likely just ran away."

Leylanda's twirling eyes focused, and they shot zingers at Wohnt. "And I suppose she removed the window by herself and set it on the ground outside her bedroom before she ran off?"

I backed out of the house, recalling the one time I'd run away from home. I was nine. My dad and mom had been fighting about him getting a job. Mom insisted he needed to get out of the house and be with people, and he said that me and Mom were already too many people for him. Well, I decided I'd make his wish come true. I packed a bag of oyster crackers, a blanket, and my favorite Judy Blume book and sneaked out, spending the night in a nearby cornfield. It was cold and scary.

When I walked back through the front door the next morning, they hadn't even noticed I'd left.

Peyton would never have run away. Leylanda was uptight and overbearing, but she cared deeply about her daughter and let her know a thousand different ways. No, Peyton wouldn't have left on her own. Right now, she was in the hands of some faceless devil. I started pacing in ever-widening circles around her house, calling her name as if she were a lost pet. The neighborhood began organizing around me.

Soon, most of Battle Lake would be searching for tiny Peyton Bertram.

Chapter 32

When I was growing up in safe, acceptably abnormal Paynesville, two things really got me keyed up. One was when it was my turn to have Connie Christopherson solve my Rubik's Cube. She was the only person in all of fifth grade who had figured it out, and she hadn't even read the book. For a small donation of Pixy Stix, she would *click-clack-click* your cube until each side was neatly monochromatic.

It was beautiful—art and organization united—and it never lasted more than one class period. It took that long to convince myself that if she could do it, I could, too. I messed it only a little bit at a time, starting by moving the middle square on all six sides. I felt confident that if I started slowly, I could find my way back.

This delusion kept Connie in Pixy Stix well into sixth grade, when the handheld Simon game and Garbage Pail Kids cards hit Paynesville via Penny Johnson's visiting cousin from Texas, effectively erasing Rubik's Cube, Snake, and Triangle from our consciousness.

The other thing that excited me was when I was allowed computer lab time. My middle school owned four Apple IIe's, and you had to be part of the gifted program to access them. The first skill we learned on the Apples was basic line programming, which involved creating a program that looked like a ball bouncing down colored stairs on the screen. I rushed to accomplish this so I could begin playing *Oregon Trail*, a control-loving girl's ticket to joy.

You started out as a pioneer about to embark on a new life in the faraway state of Oregon. The trick was, you needed to decide what to take with you to survive the journey—you had only a certain amount of space in the covered wagon and limited money to buy food, bullets, and supplies.

Your quest was played out on a maplike screen charting the wagon's progress in relation to famous towns and landmarks such as Big Hill and the Shawnakee Trading Post. Approximately ten real-life seconds after you hit the trail, one of the following would happen: (1) You would run into a buffalo stampede that you could opt to hunt, and hunting stampeding buffalo was like shooting fish in a barrel. Literally. The bullets moved with aching, underwater slowness across the green screen. (2) You would spot a group of strangers and choose how to react. "Approaching" them led to a fight, as did "circle wagons."

In either case, you needed to have your guns ready.

The game was designed to build problem-solving skills. Although I didn't see any real-world wagon train leading in my future, I derived infinite pleasure out of controlling my own destiny, if only for an hour. I acutely missed that sensation as, just before midnight, I began my trek to the public access to meet a carnival performer on the run from the law.

I had to compartmentalize Peyton's situation, tuck it away so it didn't tear through my heart and brain. If I kept imagining what she was enduring right now, I'd go mad. I'd spent four hours scouring the woods near her house for any trace of her, working with the local search party. When I'd left, a command center had been set up in front of Leylanda's with pots of coffee and doughnuts, and hundreds of flashlights stabbed the air in and around Battle Lake like fireflies. There was an audible click when I mentally separated myself from the situation, a skill I'd honed after my dad's death. *Thanks, Pops.* Footsore and heartsick, I'd left the search and gone home to change and grab my gear. Plenty of others were covering the ground. There was nothing more I could do for her tonight. I had an appointment to keep.

I knew from Sunday's post-fake-body walk that it would take me under forty-five minutes to hike to the Whiskey Lake access, and since Nikolai demanded utter stealth, walking was the way to go. I might even be able to sneak up on him and give myself the upper hand, if only for a couple moments. The slice of moon in the brilliant June sky didn't provide as much light as the twinkling stars, but between the two, I'd be able to navigate just fine, despite the exhaustion creeping into my bones. My calves ached and my shoulders were strung as tight as wings, but the discomfort felt distant, like I was walking with a borrowed body.

A rabbit darted from behind a rock and startled me, but otherwise, the landscape was serene and space-like in its starlit stillness. The only sounds were my shoes gathering dew, the far-off hum of cars cruising Highway 210, and cows lowing. The air smelled water-charged. Was a storm on the way? The keening mosquitoes were tolerable, and swooping bats feasted off the ones I didn't slap. For some reason, bats didn't bother me like birds did. Maybe it was because they were up-front about their personalities. They were leathery flying mice not trying to be anything else. Plus, anything that ate mosquitoes in Minnesota deserved respect.

When I reached the top of the sumac-speckled hill that overlooked both the public access and Shangri-La Resort, I crouched down and clicked the illuminating button on my watch. It was 11:37. I was early. Shangri-La guests were tucked in bed for the night, but nothing—not even leaves in the breeze—was moving on the peninsula. It was eerie.

The access, about two hundred yards away, was a different story. I spotted a small figure wobbling through the woods. He or she looked like a child from here, but I assumed it was Nikolai. I squinted but couldn't make out any more details except that he appeared alone.

I dropped low to the ground and crept toward him. I caught my breath behind a thick oak tree and tugged my stun gun out of the fanny pack I'd moved it to. The fanny pack was mine, but the miniature tape recorder I'd tucked in it was Sunny's. Last summer, she'd dated a guy who gaslit her. She wanted to record him before she dumped him so she could play his BS back to him. He'd thought he sounded fine. He'd gone to the curb, the tape recorder into a box marked TECHNOLOGY & JUNK.

I strapped the Z-Force to the belt of my stealth outfit—black T-shirt, black jeans with a black belt, hair pulled high in a black pony-tail holder, and black tennis shoes. I steeled myself and stole across the open expanse of the boat launch and into the edge of the woods on the other side. I counted off a hundred yards as I crept into the treed border and was only mildly frightened when a hand grabbed me.

"About time you showed up!" Nikolai hissed. His round white face glowered at me in the darkness.

"I'm early." I studied Nikolai. In the moonlit dark, his hair was a nondescript brown, and I guessed his eyes were also. He was a good-looking guy, other than the scowling. Chiseled jawline, strong nose. The top of his cranium came to boob level, which would make him a little shy of four feet. He was dressed in all black, too, and seemed injury-free and in perfect health save for a shortness of breath.

Interesting, considering the last time I'd seen him, he had appeared to be suffering from a fatal gunshot wound.

"If I've been waiting, you're not early," he snapped. "Did you bring the tape recorder?"

I patted the fanny pack. "Right here."

He was still scowling, but he wasn't going to let my supposed late-ness derail his performance. Hands on hips, he glared at me while he spoke in a tremulous voice. "Turn it on and settle back for the tale of a lifetime. It will amaze, thrill, and chill you. It will give you anticipa-tion, perspiration, and exultation. You will feel delighted, excited, and ignited. When I tell you the story of the Romanov Traveling Theater troupe, you will sigh, cry, and not want to say goodbye . . ."

That's how it went for over a half an hour, judging by the moon's location. Nikolai explained that he'd founded the troupe when he flunked out of clown school. He said he'd recruited other disenfran-chised clowns and circus acts, described what amazing acting abilities they'd cultivated; how they branched out into a carnival show to attract children, and so on.

I was just about to interrupt him when he said something that made me sit up like a dahlia in the sun: ". . . which was when I met a fellow artist like myself with really good weed. He works over at the Last Resort. I recruited him to play bongos at the Shangri-La show."

"Is this fellow artist tall with curly brown hair, and does he talk like Shaggy from *Scooby-Doo*?" I asked, already knowing the answer.

Nikolai puffed himself up at the interruption. "Yes, though that is simply one of the many faces he wears."

Jed. He *was* involved in this. My stomach bravely fought an onslaught of acid, and then surrendered to the stress in a pitiful gurgle. Was Jed just one more man who was hiding a sinister side?

Nikolai stretched and dropped his voice to a less theatrical level. "That cat has a lot of fantastic ideas. He agreed that staging my own death would be a coup de théâtre."

I doubted Jed had used those words. "Wait, you pretended to get shot for *attention*?"

"For the craft, madam, for the craft," he said impatiently. "And for a little extra cash. But you're missing the point. I had my audience spellbound. It was the greatest possible moment in live theater."

The information was coming at me fast, but he kept burying it in detail. "Extra cash?" I asked. "Someone paid you to stage your death? Who and why?"

Nikolai grinned like the Cheshire cat and rubbed his hands together. "Let's just say that a certain someone with a criminal record wanted to draw a little heat away. A harmless goal, really, but it made for spectacular theater, and now every officer in the county is looking for yours truly." He shoved his thumbs proudly into his chest. "I'm sure I would have thought of the plan on my own if he hadn't presented the idea to me."

I scoured my past conversations with Jed, trying to remember if he'd ever mentioned a criminal record. He might be goofy enough to talk Nikolai into staging his own death for a laugh, but I didn't think he was motivated enough to come up with a plan. "If *who* hadn't presented the idea to you?"

Nikolai was clearly exasperated that I kept focusing on points unrelated to him. He drew himself up to his full height. "Did Houdini tell his audience how he unlocked his chains while buried alive? Does David Copperfield reveal where his disappearing tigers go?"

Jesus, for rhetorical questions.

I needed to come at this a different way.

Chapter 33

If I could get Nikolai to reveal who had put him up to staging his own death, I'd have a better idea if Jason was my biggest problem, if he had accomplices, or whether there was someone else up to no good who I didn't even know about. I had a hunch his ego was the shortest route to the information I needed.

"How'd you fool the paramedics into thinking you'd been shot?" I asked.

He smiled arrogantly. "A stroke of genius. Let me tell you."

I didn't think I could stop him if I wanted to.

Turned out that the troupe's lizard-eyed emcee had a prescription for Guanabenz, a medication used to treat high blood pressure. A little more than the prescribed dose would slow the user's heartbeat, contract his pupils, and put him in a semicomatose state. Nikolai swallowed the Guanabenz, had the emcee shoot him with blanks, then squished some fake blood pellets over his heart. Once the paramedics established that Nikolai was stable but in serious condition, they applied pressure to the supposed chest wound and took off.

"When we reached the hospital, I jumped off the gurney in the emergency room, did my trademark tap dance to the absolute astonishment of the medical staff, and shot out the door, where the ringmaster was waiting in our tour van." He grinned. "It was beautifully executed at every point. People will be talking about it for decades."

Nikolai polished his fists on his shirt, blew on them, and beamed.

I wouldn't exactly call that plan genius. It sounded like a string of dumb-and-luck beads to me. "You know, it's illegal to use emergency services without cause."

He rolled his eyes. "Hence, you and I meeting at midnight."

That tracked. "Do you know anything about the little girl who's missing?"

Nikolai appeared genuinely surprised and wounded. "I'm an artist, not a criminal, and I don't hurt children."

The tape recorder was whirring away. "So you asked me out solely so I could write the story about your fabulous death and escape?"

"That's part of it. The important part." His voice and body seemed to shrink as he stepped outside his theater guise and became a normal guy. "The other part is I want you to get the box with the fake diamond planted in it for me. We can split the prize money seventy-thirty."

I snorted involuntarily. I hadn't seen that one coming. "Buddy, if I knew where the box was, I'd have found it by now, and I wouldn't give you any."

He nodded. "That's why you need me. I *do* know where the box is. The troupe and I were staying at a patron's acreage on the far side of this lake. I watched three folks in dive gear slip into the creek that feeds Whiskey early Monday morning. They dragged a black box tied to a rock into the lake with them." He grinned. Now that he was acting like a regular guy, his smile was endearing. "I would have missed them except that I was up early planning my death and escape."

"Why didn't you have someone from your troupe get it?"

He shrugged. "None of us knows how to dive."

I stuck my tongue in my cheek. "And how do you know *I* know how to dive?"

Nikolai laughed, then covered it with a cough. "Everyone knows that, m'dear. You're the one who got tangled up on that 'dead' body in front of Shangri-La."

"Humph." On principle, I didn't want to help him out, but there was a nice chunk of cash at stake. "Fifty-fifty."

"Sixty-forty."

"Fifty-fifty."

"Fifty-five–forty-five."

"Fifty-fifty," I said, "and you better take it, because I know where the creek is and I can just find the box all on my own now."

He held up his hands. "Okay, fifty-fifty. But you can't find the box on your own without a little bit more information." He made a criss-cross motion over his heart. "Swear you won't take more than half the reward money for that box."

I held up my right hand. "Scout's honor."

"Okay then, and that's on tape." He tapped the recorder, its tiny wheels spinning robotically in the starlight. "The reason no one has found the box yet is the divers wrapped it in a camouflage net. Their bubbles stopped about seventy-five yards straight out from the creek, so go due south from there and search for the netting." He rubbed his hands together. "Underneath that is our ticket to five thousand dollars."

A movement up the shore caught my eye. "Unless someone else finds it first." I pointed about two hundred yards east of us, where one diver was helping another into the lake, holding them and their gear close to their chest. My heartbeat lurched. Was the second diver drunk?

Nikolai chuckled softly. "Right on time. This one's on me."

I stared at him, amazed. I'd written him off as a pompous actor, but he was turning out to be so much more. I returned my attention to the two divers, just in time to see the first drop the second into the water.

Where the body began to sink, still as a corpse.

Chapter 34

From my perch on the edge of the woods, I couldn't make out the details except that both divers had their face masks on and regulators in their mouths. When the standing diver dumped the body and turned back toward the beach, the weak moonlight illuminated the writing on his wet suit's rump and the yellow tank strapped to his back. That'd weigh at least thirty pounds out of the water. That was why he was moving with all the grace of a *Land of the Lost* Sleestak.

The body he'd dropped had a yellow neoprene rope dragging from it, exactly like the one I'd stumbled into near the moose skeleton. The wheels were turning. I was about to make the connection when the diver stopped to look back at the body he'd dumped, removing his face mask to rub at his eyes.

Jed.

My breath caught. The form he'd dumped had to be another bogus body, right? No normal human could lift a full-suited person while fully outfitted themselves.

Jed was planting fake bodies, and I might know why.

I was still hoping for more information from Nikolai, though he was proving to be craftier than I'd given him credit for. Playing dumb seemed like the best route. "What's happening down there?" I whispered.

"You'll have to get the combination for that safe on your own, dear," he said, chuckling. "I'm done for the night. I'll meet you back here tomorrow to claim my half of the reward. Same time, same rules."

He melted into the woods, but I was no longer paying attention.

I wasn't thinking about who'd convinced him to pretend to die.

I wasn't even—for a blessed moment—thinking about Peyton.

I was having a real, honest-to-goodness, light-bulb-sparking-over-my-head epiphany.

You'll have to get the combination for that safe on your own, dear.

Nikolai's words had been offhand for him, a klieg light for me. *Of course.* Regina's code numbers were the combination to a safe: 23 left, 12 right, 11 left. Cosmic duh! I just had to find out what she'd meant by the kissing tree, and I'd have the jewels.

I considered racing back to my house and calling the police to tell them someone was planting another body in the lake, but I had a heavy feeling that Jed wouldn't get treated well by law enforcement. Plus, I didn't want to pull any person power away from the search for Peyton.

I hiked back to my house, glanced wistfully at my bed through the window, and drove to town to crash on Gina's couch.

Chapter 35

I slept poorly, the few hours of sleep I managed to scratch out punctuated by nightmares of Peyton on a fiery roller coaster. I woke around nine, tired and crabby, Tiger Pop curled up on my feet and Luna snuffling at my ear. I took patient Luna for a long walk, deflating when I saw the town was wallpapered with posters of the missing seven-year-old.

The Channel 5 News crew was in front of the bank, interviewing a Woodlawn Resort employee. I heard her say she was one of the coordinators of the local search party and that they'd gotten up early to look.

"We're not going to stop until we find our girl," she said firmly. The camera lights glinted off the "Find Peyton" button on her chest, and she stared into the camera when she spoke. Small towns had big hearts for their kids.

I snuffed the guilt bubble growing in me. I shouldn't have slept at all last night. I should have hunted for Peyton. But what could I do that the whole town wasn't already doing? My time was best spent getting my hands on those jewels and nailing Jason.

That's what I told myself. It was easier than acknowledging the truth: I was terrified for Peyton, my insides scraped raw with worry. And if I thought about it too much, it would crack through every wall I'd built since my father died.

No, I needed to stay busy to stay sane.

I returned Luna to Gina's, took a quick shower and snarfed down a cold cheese sandwich, and made it to the library just in time to open at ten. Mrs. Berns was waiting outside. She was wearing a fuchsia running suit, which was ironic, since the only exercise she got didn't require clothes.

"You look like warm barf," she told me. "You sleepin' okay?"

I turned the key and heard the tumbler click. Peyton's face was staring sweetly back at me from the flyer taped to the door. "Matter of fact, I'm not, Mrs. Berns. My life has been a little hectic lately."

In addition to my worries for Peyton, my race to find the jewels, my investigative reporting, and my now-full-time library job, I also had two dear animals, a large lawn, and flower and vegetable gardens that I was neglecting.

My life was running away without me.

"Figured. Here's my résumé. I'm your new part-time librarian."

I glanced at the handwritten sheet of lined notebook paper she'd shoved into my face, the confetti edges still hanging on where she'd ripped it from a spiral tablet. In the center of the page, she had scribbled, *My name is Mrs. Berns, and I'm your new assistant librarian.*

Concise.

I grimaced. "I don't know if we have the budget for another librarian."

She waggled her finger. "You had enough money for you and Lartel, that swishy-pant-wearing freak, so you have enough money for you and me. You tell me if you got someone better begging for this job."

She had a point. The line of people who wanted to sit indoors on a beautiful Minnesota summer day for minimum wage was only slightly longer than the line of Otter Tail County men who wanted to enter counseling to improve their personal relationships. Besides, I could use more hours in my day, and I didn't have a better plan for getting them. I sighed. "Fine. I'll hire you on a trial basis. If you work out, I'll set you up for regular hours."

She clapped her hands and then rubbed them together. "You're a smart girl. The first thing we're going to do is get an adult section in here. All these namby-pamby books are a good front, but we know what people really want to read. And in back, we'll add a smoking room to draw the bar crowd. And this carpeting—"

"No! No changes!" I rubbed the bridge of my nose. "If you're going to work here, you have to remember that I'm the boss. This is the public library, not a pleasure palace." She followed me into the foyer. "You can start by shelving those books in the drop-off bin." I pointed at the box.

She scowled at me, arms crossed, but after a few seconds, she gave in and grabbed the books. I sensed that this was the calm before the storm, and she was gathering strength for a later confrontation.

Until then, I planned to enjoy the help.

◆ ◆ ◆

Mrs. Berns turned out to be an astonishingly efficient coworker when she wasn't reading over patrons' shoulders or whistling at the male clientele. With her help, the library was in better shape than it had been since I'd started in April. It was an hour before closing, and there was nothing left to do.

"Why don't you go home, dear," Mrs. Berns suggested when she caught me at the front counter staring toward the door. "I'll get these people out of here and lock up."

The offer was tempting. She'd already worked alone at the library once and had not burned it down. I was itching to talk to Jed, and I also needed to walk Luna and then run home to water my garden and mow my lawn before it became a wood tick sanctuary.

I just didn't know about leaving Mrs. Berns with the keys. She had a history of raucous, racy behavior. I needed to behave responsibly. "I only have the one key, and the city council gave me strict instructions not to lend it out when they hired me."

She dug around in her white plastic purse and came out with a rapper-size key ring. She methodically clinked through the metal passports. "Municipal liquor store, high school, cop shop . . . here it is! The Battle Lake Public Library. Looks like we're set."

I was astounded. "How'd you get keys to all those places?"

She winked. "A woman's wiles. Plus, it's sort of a hobby of mine."

The realization that Mrs. Berns had probably already spent a lot of time alone in the library was oddly liberating. "It's a deal. Close it up at the top of the hour, and I'll meet you back here tomorrow morning at ten so we can draw up your schedule."

"You got it, homey." She threw me some Midwestern nursing home sign—it looked like someone giving themselves a shot followed by a thumbs-up—before heading to the stacks. I snatched my purse from behind the counter. It contained the recording of Nikolai's story, and I wanted to listen to it on my drive to see if I had missed any clues. I was only ten minutes in when I pulled up to the Last Resort. For the first time, I noticed that a cabin's roof was sagging and the boat tied to the dock had seen better days.

Sal was working in the office. She directed me to the hammock tied between two trees near the beach. That's where I found Jed snoozing, wearing nothing but bright-aqua Bermuda shorts. He had a fresh bandage wrapped around his knee. I prodded him gently.

He snorted, stretched, and opened one eye. "Whaddya know for sure?" His wide smile was sincere.

"Not much these days." I smiled back, but it hurt. If he was working with Jason, or something worse, I was about to hear it. "Your knee looks a little rough. What'd you do to it?"

He pushed himself to a seated position and rubbed the swollen area around the bandage. "I scraped it on a rock, diving."

I sighed. "When you first lent me the dive equipment, you said you twisted it unloading a boat and that you hadn't been diving in a while."

He glanced at me once, quickly, and his cheeks flushed. "Yeah, I musta forgot." He studied his nails. "You know, it'd be great to find that box."

"It sure would be nice to have some extra money to fix up this place, wouldn't it?" I rubbed my chin like I was thinking. "Business has been kinda slow here, according to Sal."

Jed nodded solemnly, and then his face brightened. "But it's already getting better. What with that fake dead body in front of Shangri-La, and then the shooting, not as many people want to stay there anymore. We're full up for the first time in three summers."

Sweet Jed, as transparent as Saran Wrap. Relief washed over me. He wasn't evil. The opposite, really. He'd been trying to save his family business. "I know you planted that dummy that I found in Whiskey and another one last night."

His eyes grew big like fried eggs, the wheels turning as he struggled to find a way out of this. Unfortunately, all the pot had rusted his cogs. A big, shiny tear formed at the corner of each eye. "Mira, I feel so crappy about that. I really do, man, and I know my karma is going to be subpar. But I had to help my parents. I had to! I suppose you're gonna turn me into the Man?"

I wanted to comfort him, but first, I had to be sure. "What do you know about Jason Blunt?"

"Nothing, except he was a supreme toker back in high school. That dude would do any drug you passed him." Jed smiled happily at the memory. "A little bit of a temper, but otherwise fun."

"Is he involved in any of this?" I asked.

Jed looked puzzled. "Planting those two bodies to scare people off Whiskey Lake was my idea, Mira. Nobody else even knows I did it."

Except for me and Nikolai. Jed wouldn't be earning his "stealthy" badge anytime soon. "Then why'd you tell me that Jason rented some dive suits from you?"

He shrugged, palms up. "It was the only name I could think of when you asked me." His face was so open that I believed him. He tossed his curls out of his eyes. "How'd you figure out it was me underwater surfing the bodies?"

"Mostly dumb luck." I was crunching my options. "How about this—I'll make a deal with you. You stop selling pot, stop planting bodies, and stop hanging out with actors and carnival folk, and I won't tell on you."

"Can I still *smoke* pot?"

I held out my hand. "Until your head starts on fire."

"Deal!" He shook my hand enthusiastically, wiggling like a puppy. He'd been harboring guilt about his dead-body missions, and I'd absolved him.

"I gotta go mow my lawn now," I said. "You stay out of trouble."

He started to pull himself out of the hammock but winced when he tried bending his bad leg. "I can mow your lawn. I do all our grass here."

I'll bet. "That's okay, buddy. I need the downtime to think through some things. You get that knee looked at, all right?"

He nodded. "My mom's taking me to the doctor tomorrow."

"Good." I was about to leave when I thought of one more thing. "You don't have a criminal record, do you?"

"Not me, but I do think I'm being watched." He glanced around for effect. "I can feel it. Makes my baby hairs stand up sometimes."

I smiled. He was just high, dopey Jed. He hadn't arranged for anyone to pretend to get shot. He couldn't even arrange to bring himself to the doctor. "Thanks, Jed." I hugged him before trotting back to my car. One mystery solved. I loved tying up loose ends, although I still didn't have the jewels or know where Peyton was.

And I'd begun to have a nagging suspicion the two were connected.

Chapter 36

I splayed my fingers outside my window as I drove, riding the air like waves. When my radio crackled out a recognizable version of 4 Non Blondes' "What's Up," I chanted along in my tinny, off-key singing voice. I loved it when meteorological forces converged to send me a decent radio signal.

I pulled into my driveway and quickly checked my house for vandalism or excrement. I had about four hours of daylight left and a lot to do. The double-wide seemed untouched, so I watered my plants and checked my caller ID. No one had reached out, not even a telemarketer. I felt a little bit sorry for myself, but quickly dismissed that.

I wasn't lonely, I was alone. There was nothing wrong with that.

Not that it hadn't occurred to me more than once that a government-sponsored dating program wouldn't be a welcome addition to the tax rolls. I was a cynic about men, but I never stopped hoping that there were some good ones out there. I just didn't have the time or patience to sift through the chaff looking for them.

I had a theory that if Big Brother got involved, the whole process could be streamlined. When a person turned eighteen, they would sign up for the Selective Service. (The military would have to get a new name for their deal, since "Selective Service" was too perfect for a dating organization.) Entrants would have to enter and keep current basic information—education level, one joke they considered funny, profession, whether they liked or wanted kids, why their last relationship ended, et cetera. They'd also have to provide at least three previous relationship testimonials.

Not only would this hold us more accountable in how we behaved with current partners—because we knew the person we were with today could be writing a dating reference for us tomorrow—it would also provide a database of people who were single and looking not to be, thus broadening our search area. After all, what were the odds of your soulmate living within sixty miles of where you were now, and of accidentally running into them in some leg of your daily routine?

I wondered how one would go about getting legislation like that passed. I'd have to add it to my to-do list. I already had my screen name picked out: Pink and Suspicious.

Meanwhile, I had some lawn to mow. I'd always liked cutting the grass. The hum and snort of the engine was soothing, and the results were organizationally breathtaking, particularly on this property, with the rolling hills and sprawling trees. It would give me some downtime to organize my thoughts on the jewels and Peyton.

I switched to jogging shorts and a tank top and trotted down to the red shed where I housed the mower. I gassed up the old Snapper rider, checked the oil, and cleaned the area around the blade. I also loop-knotted my purse to the square handlebars so I could bring the recording of Nikolai and give it another listen once I found my rhythm. I revved up the mower and started juicing grass, missing the familiar form of Luna jogging alongside.

I couldn't wait to move me and my animals back here.

I jostled and purred over the lawn in front of the house, being careful to reverse direction when I rode close to my gardens so I wouldn't shoot weed seeds into them. While steering, I held the tape recorder to my ear and listened to the rest of the interview. Nothing caught my attention, though it confirmed what I already knew—that Jed was the body planter and neither he nor Nikolai knew what'd happened to Peyton. I regassed after about an hour and a half of mowing and moved to the area between the barn and sheds.

When I finished, the mosquitoes and gnats were circling like sharks and the sun was setting, drawing shades of lavender across the horizon. I puttered the mower back into the shed and stretched, my legs shaky from three hours on a vibrating vehicle. I started to untie my purse when it occurred to me that I hadn't mowed the little patch of lawn down along the shoreline that led to Shangri-La. I hated backtracking, but it would be a nice feeling of completion to have it all freshly cut.

I left my purse untied on my lap and cruised down the driveway, bumping along the gravel. The trees formed a natural archway, and the fairy light of dusk shimmered through the leaves and made the path surreal. I could smell pollen in the air, and despite all the stress and fear weighing me down, it felt good to be outdoors, tending to the earth.

When I reached my destination, I killed the motor to pick up a Diet Coke can and a bunch of candy wrappers that had been tossed into the grass, probably left by folks going to or fleeing from the party on the peninsula. I glanced into the deepening woods, away from Shangri-La, to where I'd been carried during the magic show. Suddenly curious to check if the bongo-slash-chariot was still there, I tracked through the trees and brush, prickly ash and raspberry branches grabbing at me.

I realized I was still holding my purse and the garbage I'd gathered, so I shoved the wrappers into my bag, crinkling a stack of construction paper. It was the pictures Peyton had given me—one of the house, one of the animal, and one of her studying.

All my efforts to keep thoughts of her tucked away were destroyed as I looked at the sweet, scribbled drawings. Tears clouded my eyes. I traced my fingers over the wobbly letters spelling out "math lab," something nagging at me, telling me I was overlooking something big. What, I couldn't get at. It was a dark and liquid shape moving in and out of the fog, offering me only glimpses.

I shook my head, stashed the drawings back in the purse, and slid the strap over my shoulder, freeing my hands to push aside branches. The setting sun was turning the forest shadows sinister. I kept thinking

I saw someone out of the corner of my eye, but when I'd turn, no one was there. The birds began making a different sound, too, a warning warble that rolled down my spine like ice.

By the time I reached the drop-off spot, it was all I could do not to turn around and run, but I refused to let fear control me on my own property. Well, my borrowed property. I belonged here. I was safe. Other than being kidnapped and tossed out here, that was. I looked around. The bongo was gone. In fact, there was no sign anyone had recently visited this clearing. I knew it was the right spot only because of the intertwined elms I'd noticed when I'd shot out of my cage, the trees that looked like two people making out.

My heartbeat paused, and then came crashing back as the realization hit: *this* must be the kissing tree I'd been searching for! Of course it would be close to Shangri-La.

I dug in my purse and tugged out Ron's translation, my hands shaking:

With your back to the kissing tree walk seven steps northwest kneel 23 left 12 right 11 left.

I backed up against the kissing elm and shimmied around until I was facing northwest. I walked seven long steps and knelt. On my right was an oak tree and on my left was a rise covered in rotting leaves and poison ivy. Son of a monkey! For all I knew, the rise was nothing but dirt, or maybe a rusting piece of farm machinery, a common sight in Minnesota woods. Were the potential jewels enough reason to dig in a poison ivy nest?

Not bare-handed, certainly.

My best bet would be to run to the house and fetch a long-sleeved shirt and some gardening gloves, but I didn't have the patience for that, and besides, it'd be dark soon. I scoured around the forest floor until I found a nice long stick and returned to poke at the pile. My stick hit something beneath the plants, the *scritch scritch* of wood on metal.

My pulse leaped. The pile was more than simply dirt.

Was it hidden jewels?

I hooked the stick onto a long vine and yanked, hoping to remove enough poison ivy that I could get at what was underneath. Just brushing against the plant would result in a severe rash that'd itch so bad you'd consider getting skinned alive just to make it stop. While I was able to lift a chunk of ivy, it revealed about twenty feet of hairy roots spreading in each direction, all of it dripping with poisonous resin.

The devil plant wasn't going anywhere.

I dropped the branch and calculated how long it would take to reach the lake to rinse off the poisonous resin if I just dived into the pile real quick, just long enough to peek at what had made the metal noise. I had the trip clocked at about two minutes. Once in the lake, I could use the sand to scour the poison off my skin.

That would keep it from infecting me, right?

I knelt and was stretching my hand toward the noxious vine when voices drifted down the road from Shangri-La. I cocked my ear, my blood turning to ice.

It was Sam and Jason.

And by the sound of it, they'd stepped off the road and were entering the forest, headed straight for me.

Chapter 37

I had three options: flee, hide, or stroll toward them, acting like I was just hanging in the woods, no big. I doubted I could outrun Jason, and I figured I could always try the strolling thing if hiding didn't work, so I darted to a nearby tree, crouching and hugging my back to the oak. My heart was hammering like a hummingbird's, fear making it difficult to draw a full breath as Jason's voice came close enough to make out what he was saying.

"What sort of dumb bitch leaves a lawn mower out? She could at least finish the job."

"Maybe she just stopped to take a leak."

"Maybe I'll put a leak in her head if I come across her."

I bit my lip and felt my eyes grow hot. At least I had my purse, which meant I had Z-Force. I reached in, careful not to crinkle the paper inside and draw attention to myself. I felt the stun gun's hard plastic and slowly drew out my weapon.

I glanced down, gratitude turning to frustration. *I grabbed the tape recorder, not Z-Force!* I almost tossed the recorder back in, but instead set it on the ground, timing my movement with Jason's and Sam's footsteps so I hit the record button when their noise would disguise it. If they were going to maul me, at least it would be on tape for some savvy police officer to find. Maybe, in an absurd punch line to my life, Ody and Gary could stumble across it in some flurry of teamwork, saying they knew me when.

I settled the recorder next to a large, gnarled root, turned the volume knob on high, quietly covered the unit with rotting leaves, and dug into my purse. This time I found the prize: little Z-Force, which had worked well on Jed and his accomplice. It felt good cradled in my hand. I steadied my shaky breath and concentrated on making myself disappear.

Chapter 38

"Who told you that's what the code says?" Jason's voice sounded about twenty feet away. Judging by the twitchy edge to his tone, he was tweaking or he was angry. Maybe both. Jed hadn't mentioned Jason doing coke, but it wouldn't surprise.

"Some old couple back at the Resort," Sam said. "I saw them doing a crossword and asked them if they'd solve a puzzle for me. They knew right away what it was." I sensed pride in her voice, but it was lost on Jason.

"A steaming pile of bullshit, that's what it is," he said, talking too fast. "I can't believe that dumbass hid a heap of jewelry in the woods and then left some secret message to find it in an invisible room. Moron."

Sam sounded defensive. "She wasn't a total idiot, just a little eccentric. What's a rich lady supposed to do with a bunch of stolen jewelry, anyhow? She couldn't wear it, and she couldn't sell it with it being so hot. She just never got around to coming back for it. Anyhow, that leaves it all for us."

They were about fifteen feet away now, and they'd stopped. I guessed they were near the kissing tree. I prayed that Jason knew which way was northwest and didn't accidentally lurch across me. Outside the woods, the sun was still halfway above the horizon, but in the forest, there was more shadow than light.

I tried to calm myself with the hope that the darker it grew, the harder I would be to see, but the more I focused on breathing, the more difficult it became to breathe at all. Jason was scary enough when he was regular angry. What would he be like hopped up?

"Okay, walk seven steps northwest," he commanded. "I'm sure it's seven *girl* steps."

"Which way is northwest?" Sam asked.

I could almost hear him point, the tension dripping in the air. The crunching sound of her walking over fallen sticks came next.

Jason's voice was sharp. "You see anything?"

"Gawd, Jason, you're right behind me. *You* see anything? Huh?" Her New York accent was extra thick, and her gum snapped in the air. "Like that big pile under the weeds? Duh?"

There was the smack of hard skin on soft, and Sam yelped. My fear was pushed aside by rage. He must have slapped her.

"Hold this," he growled.

A moment of silence was followed by the sound of roots being plucked and dirt being moved. A smile pushed at my lips. Could it be? Did Jason not recognize the poison ivy?

"What do you see?" Sam's voice was overly light, likely reflecting her worry that questioning him would upset him again. "Is it the safe?"

"It's the size of Fort Knox." Jason laughed, more startled than happy. "How did the old bag drag this out here?"

"She talked her husband into borrowing a dolly and moving it right before the Addamses sold the place, but she never told me where he moved it to." Her voice was still high, singsongy. "Said he'd buried everything but the face of it."

"Crazy bitch."

"Yeah, crazy bitch." Sam laughed, sounding almost girlish.

"It's a good thing you got that job, honey." Jason was sunshine and roses now that he was about to get his hands on treasure. "Can you shine that light over here? I got the lock uncovered."

Suddenly the forest was lit up. They must have brought a torch light. I felt big and obvious and ground my shoulder blades into the tree. I even considered closing my eyes on the time-honored principle that if you can't see them, they can't see you. Instead, I wiped my sweating hands one by one on my shorts.

"What's the code, baby?" Jason asked.

Paper crinkled. "Twenty-three left, twelve right, eleven left. Is it turning okay?"

"Not hardly. Hand me the weasel piss." A squirting sound like juicy hair spray was followed by the whirring of a lock turning. "There she is!"

"Lemme see!"

"Back off!" Jason barked. "Give me that light!"

The groan of a long-closed door creaking open pierced the air, followed immediately by Sam's scream. A disorienting flash of brightness and then dark told me she'd dropped the light.

"There's a body in there!" she shrieked.

"A corpse can't hurt you," Jason growled. The brightness from the flashlight steadied, and I heard the grunt of a laugh. "Geez, I can't believe he still smells. There's even some body juice in here yet. Must be the old bag's husband."

Sam retched. "That reeks. How come he's not just bones?"

"I dunno, maybe it was airtight? Get out of my way so I can move it." He whistled. "Your old boss sure was a piece of work. She makes her husband drag the safe out so she can hide her stolen jewels, and then she buries him inside. Real nice. The old coot deserved what she got."

"She didn't deserve to be murdered," Sam said quietly. "She was an old lady, not hurting anyone anymore. She wasn't going to live much longer anyhow."

"She was a crook and a murderer," Jason said, laughing darkly. A moist thump told me he'd dropped the body. Dude really was touching everything he could without gloves. "I think the two of us would've gotten along just fine."

"If you hadn't killed her," Sam said.

"Shut your piehole," Jason said, but the anger was gone from his voice. His focus was elsewhere. "Why can't you let anything drop? What the . . . here it is!"

"What?"

"Look at this pile!" Jason's tone was laced with wonder as prisms of red, green, and purple reflected off the leaves. "Would you look at it? Jesus. It's like a goddamn pirate's treasure."

The temptation was too much. I peered around the corner of my hiding tree, hopeful that Jason would be too distracted by the jewels to notice any movement in the darkening woods.

I was right.

He was in profile, kneeling over a rotting cloth bag, all but drooling as he stared inside. Sam was leaning over his shoulder and shining the light inside the bag, causing the sparkling colors to dance off their faces. A dark crumple of a shape lay nearby. The body technically could be anyone, but given that Mrs. Krupps's husband had disappeared about the same time she left the area, it was a safe bet that Jason was right and the corpse was indeed Bradford Krupps. The sweet, poisonous smell of rotted flesh wafted over to me.

"Can I touch them?" Sam asked.

"You can wear 'em, baby!" He spanked a tiara on her head, and she performed a beauty queen walk straight out of a Miss America pageant. Jason nodded approvingly, fondling the gems in the bag. "This is just the beginning, baby. We invest these in the rest of the equipment we need to get the meth lab going, and we'll never have to work another day in our lives. Hot damn, we can probably hire people to run the lab for us!"

The dark, liquid shape finally stepped out of the mental fog.

Peyton standing behind Jason as he talked on his cell phone at the turtle races. Her math lab drawing afterward—only it wasn't a *math* lab, it was a *meth* lab. The term would have no meaning for a little girl, so she'd reworked it into something familiar.

Jason must have discovered she knew about the lab and snatched her.

My armor fell away. I didn't care about the jewels if I could save Peyton. Hot tears ran down my cheeks. I needed to get out of here immediately to tell the police. I was calculating my quietest, quickest route to the station when a swallow flew into the oak tree two over from where I was hiding. Either those birds were the Jerry Lewises of the avian world, or else I emitted some disorienting signal that only swallows could hear.

I bit my lip.

The bird's impact had made a tiny noise, more like the pop of a knuckle than the bang of a collision, but it'd been enough to burn the smile from Jason's voice and force him to his feet. "If any-goddamn-body is hiding over there, they have one chance to speak, or I will make sure they forever hold their peace!"

The fear was so strong I nearly gagged, but I had to keep my head if I was going to escape, and I had to get out of here if I was going to save Peyton. I slowly levered myself up using only my feet and the tree. I carefully tilted my purse off my shoulder and gently rested it on the ground to increase my aerodynamics. The zapper I kept clutching in my right hand.

I was going to run.

But Jason was tromping toward me, scratching himself. The poison was beginning its assault on his skin. "Fe, fi, fo, fum, I smell the blood of somebody whose ass I'm gonna kick!"

I had an inappropriate, crazy urge to pee or sing. As he approached on my left, I wiggled around to the right, staying just out of his peripheral vision. I was a quarter of the way around when Sam shrieked. "There's someone behind that tree!"

I charged out from my not-so-hidden spot and beat cheeks for the road. The nearer I could get to Shangri-La, the better my chances of attracting enough attention to stop Jason.

And if I didn't escape these woods, Peyton was as good as dead.

Chapter 39

There were about a hundred feet of forest between me and the road, and I devoured them like a starving woman at a smorgasbord.

Unfortunately, Jason was hungrier than me.

He grabbed my ponytail, snapping my head back before I covered even twenty feet. He whipped me around until we were face-to-face and slapped me openhanded. The force turned everything into a blank. I tasted blood as I crumpled to the forest floor, my stun gun lost. Jason kicked me in the stomach, and my diaphragm locked up, unable to pull in air.

Peyton.

I thought I heard Sam screaming.

"That good enough for you, Mira?" He towered over me, his voice jarringly calm. "You think I'm insane? You think I'm a crazy man? Some of us hide it good, like old lady Krupps, and some of us don't, but we all got it. And now it's your turn to get it."

He kicked some dirt in my face, blinding me. I dragged myself away from the sound of his voice, bumping up against a tree. I struggled to sit up. I felt nauseated and my mouth was salty with blood, but there was surprisingly little pain. I stole bits of air as my diaphragm spasmed.

"Where you going in such a hurry?" Jason was saying. "We've saved a little room here for you. Your new home. Sam, prepare the safe." When I realized that he meant to toss me inside, I threw up, not able to swallow it back before it leaked out the corners of my mouth.

I was beyond terrified.

Jason was going to bury me alive, and there was no one to stop him. I tried to scurry away, but Jason pulled me back, whipping me around so he could slap me again. He was crouched close to me, his pupils dilated and twitching, spittle glinting on his chin.

"Bastard," I grunted.

"What's that, Mira?" He held his hand to his ear, his gesture exaggerated, comical. "You got something to say to me?"

A picture of Peyton formed in my mind, smiling up at me as I read her *Prince Cinders*. We were both safe in the children's section of the library, far from this madman. I concentrated on this image to remain conscious and reached deep into my reserves.

I started crawling again.

Another kick landed on my ribs. Somewhere Sam was pleading, but Jason wasn't listening.

"Let's end this," he was saying to me. "You and me, Mira. Let's put it to bed."

I'd begun crawling again. My hand connected with a rock about the size of a grapefruit. The one eye that could open told me that the rock was white. I hoped it wasn't too obvious in the dark. I dug at it, peeling my fingernails back in my desperation to hold it.

"Shut up, Sam!" he yelled at her before turning back to me. "You have any last words before you go to sleep forever?" he asked, his voice close to my ear. He was kneeling beside me.

I turned my heavy head toward him. "Yeah," I croaked. "You're a pathetic bastard, and no one will ever respect you."

At least that's what I said in my head. The reality was that I was focusing all my fading consciousness on the rock.

I slammed it into his face.

He tumbled back, grunting in surprise. I took advantage, levering myself off the ground with a burst of adrenaline. Using both hands, I brought the rock down on his head, all the anger and loneliness that I'd gathered in my lifetime joining with my fears for a little girl who was terrified and was me.

I believe if I'd connected directly with his head, I would have split it in two, spilling his brains onto the forest floor. I would have been fine with that. As it was, he turned at the last second. The rock glanced the edge of his forehead with enough force to peel off a chunk of skin. His eyes widened in surprise, fogged over, and then closed.

I swayed over him for a moment, watching the leaves nearest his mouth flutter with his breath. Blood gushed out of his head wound. I staggered back and stared wildly around for more attackers.

Sam was leaning against the kissing tree, her face stained with tears. She pulled an Eve Slim out of her shorts pocket with shaking hands and lit it.

"Wanna split the jewels?" she asked.

I couldn't for the life of me recall what she was talking about, but if I knew one thing, it was that I wasn't in a sharing mood. "No."

She sighed. "Didn't think so."

She brushed off her behind and strolled back the way she'd come. I scrabbled in the near dark for the tape recorder and then limped after her, accidentally kicking the stun gun. I leaned over to grab it, the exertion shooting needles of pain through my bruised torso, and limped back to Jason.

I zapped him once. His body spasmed and he groaned, but his breathing stayed constant.

It was a crying shame.

Chapter 40

I hobbled out of the woods and toward Shangri-La, thinking about how stupid Jason was.

He'd seen the secret room and decided it would be a perfect spot for a meth lab, probably for all the same reasons the original architect had thought it would make an ideal rum room. Fair enough. But once he discovered the jewels, *millions of dollars' worth of jewels*, he still intended to start a meth lab.

That lack of imagination told me he was likely using the same room to hide Peyton.

If she was still alive.

Every step I took attacked my head like knives. I wouldn't have made it if a couple out walking hadn't seen me stumble from the woods. The woman wanted me to rest while the man ran back to Shangri-La to call the police. He promised me he'd look for Peyton in the main bedroom closet the minute he got off the phone, but no way could I wait here if Peyton was there. I made the woman help me back. When she went too slow, I speed-limped away from her, using the fumes in my tank to haul myself up the stairs.

Guests were gathering around the bedroom door, which Kellie had unlocked.

I pushed past Kellie, past the man who had promised me he'd called the police, all the way into the closet, which none of them had yet entered. My throat was raw, my body so bruised I couldn't stand up straight, one eye entirely swollen shut. I must have looked like a monster crawling through that hole.

My flashlight was still at my waist. When I reached for it, I realized I had at least one sprained finger. I clicked the light on with my ring finger, my heart in my throat.

"Peyton?" I rasped.

At first, I saw only the still. The propane tank.

No Peyton.

For a moment, the world exploded in pain so fierce that I was worried it would erase me. But then I spotted the juice box on its side. And a pair of sneakers attached to little-girl legs on the bottom of a little-girl body beneath the sweetest little-girl face I'd ever seen.

"Peyton!" I screamed.

She was alive, bound and gagged, her eyes crusted with tears, but otherwise unharmed. Stronger hands pushed past me to untie her. When she was free, she ran to me. I held her tight, smelling her sweet shampoo, not releasing her until Leylanda arrived.

Chapter 41

The police beat the ambulance. When I gave Gary a rundown on what had just happened, including the dead body in the safe ("No, I know. But this one really is dead."), the feds were called in. Unfortunately, the press wasn't far behind, so several grotesque pictures of me were snapped before the paramedics whisked me off to the hospital. I made some crack that they better not lose me like they did the circus performer.

They didn't laugh.

Luckily, the photos of me never made it into any paper. I was pushed aside for pictures of the joyful reunion between Peyton and Leylanda.

At the hospital, my X-rays showed a mild concussion, severe bruising, three sprained fingers, but no broken bones. Eating mostly carbohydrates really did pay off. Jason was still unconscious when he was loaded into the second ambulance and driven to the hospital. Like me, he had a concussion, plus he needed seven stitches in his head.

That made me the winner.

As a sweet bonus, Jason also had the worst case of poison ivy on record in the five-state area. He required prednisone shots to keep his throat from closing up and had to have his hands strapped down to keep from scratching. They even took photos of his full-body, oozing sores to use in some medical textbook.

When I handed my tape recording of Jason confessing to killing Regina over to the police, he was pretty much assured of some jail time for murder, but Samantha Beladucci, a.k.a. Sam Krupps, cemented that reality. When the state police caught her about to cross into Wisconsin, she cooperated fully. She'd likely serve some time for aiding and abetting, but Jason was going away for a long, long time.

Sam's story proved it had gone down just like I'd thought. Regina had stolen the jewels and then hidden them in the safe in the woods, planning to come back for them at a future date. Autopsy results showed her husband had taken a severe blow to the head, but the actual cause of death was inconclusive due to the age of the remains. It was safe to assume that Regina had killed him.

If she was wild enough to knock off her husband, she was certainly irrational enough to leave a wealth of jewels hidden in rural Minnesota, which made me wonder what my stash of rhinestones said about my mental health.

But I saw no reason to dwell on that.

And, of course, the whole fiasco came home to roost when Regina blabbed the story to Sam, her nurse, who then told it to Jason, who she'd met in a casino in upstate New York. Good-looking, flattering, liked to have a good time.

She swore she never imagined he'd murder Regina.

The *Pioneer Press* contest had been an unhappy coincidence. Jason had found out about it when he called to reserve the deluxe room at Shangri-La. Kellie Gibson had assumed he was getting a head start on the contest and had asked him about it. He played along like that was his real reason, but he was fuming at the attention and number of people it would bring, particularly since, according to Sam, he'd just been released from jail in Texas for possession of methamphetamines and wasn't supposed to leave the state.

Kellie had inadvertently provided a distraction for Jason's nefarious jewel hunting when she booked the Romanov troupe. When Jason approached Nikolai for help scaring me off and drawing heat away from the peninsula, Nikolai had been more than happy to help, once

Jason assured him no one would really get hurt and that it'd be great publicity for the troupe.

Meanwhile, Jason tore apart the bedroom closet and discovered the secret room right away. When he couldn't find any clues that would lead him to the safe, he decided to make lemonade out of lemons and began to gather what he needed to start a meth lab. He knew the resort was empty in the off-season, with the Gibsons flying down to Arizona every winter. The rum room would be perfect for manufacturing meth, a lucrative enterprise in a remote location.

The hitch came when, at the turtle races, Peyton overheard him talking to a friend about what he'd need to start his own operation, and she'd kept asking him what a "math lab" was. Once Jason realized he could lose the jewels *and* the dream of his own meth lab if she told her mom, he decided to silence her.

Sam wasn't keen on the idea of killing a kid, though. She convinced Jason to wait until the box in Whiskey Lake was found. She'd argued that once the excitement died down, there would be a lot fewer people and photographers around, and it would be a lot easier to dispose of her body.

Jason agreed.

Sam swore she'd just been buying time to figure out how to set Peyton free.

Meanwhile, Jason knew I'd taken something out of the hidden room. He nabbed the code from me at the turtle races. When Sam got the couple at Shangri-La to crack it, he'd known exactly what "the kissing tree" was since he had spent a lot of time hunting in Sunny's woods and even had a stand nearby.

And the rest of it I caught on tape.

Sam went on the record vehemently denying that they'd planted the fake body in the lake or shot Nikolai. That was one mystery the police would never solve because I saw no payoff in tattling, only downsides. I reminded myself to have Jed remove the second fake body, the one he'd planted last night, before someone stumbled across it.

I spent twenty-four hours in the hospital.

Someone had called Gina, who picked me up. She said I could stay at her place as long as I wanted. I was grateful for the offer, but I couldn't reclaim Luna and Tiger Pop and head back to my place fast enough.

Sleeping in my own bed for the first time in days was glorious, bruises and sprains notwithstanding. I was naked and comfortable, Tiger Pop purring away between my feet.

I'd missed the window for diving for the box and splitting the reward with Nikolai, but there was nothing I could do about that. I don't know if he showed up at our designated spot, because I never heard from him again.

Probably there was a theatrical Romanov somewhere cursing my name right now.

Chapter 42

Once I was back on my feet, I stopped by the library only long enough to ask Mrs. Berns if she'd mind if I took the day off. She happily agreed to hold down the fort whenever I needed it. Unfortunately, she was wearing a skirt with slits nearly to her armpits when she told me.

Fortunately, she had great legs.

Still, my first order of business was to track down Kennie and hire her to tell Mrs. Berns that she must dress more professionally at the library. As an afterthought, I also asked her to "pull a Jason" on Leif, Gina's husband. Kennie was to go to Clyde's, where Leif got fall-down drunk most weekends, and then lure him out to her car, where she'd take pictures of him wearing "I Love PETA" and "Vegans forever" signs. I encouraged her to enlist Mrs. Berns's help in this endeavor.

"Don't actually *do* anything to him, Kennie," I clarified. "I just need the pictures for blackmail, something to keep him honest."

"Sure, I won't actually *do* anything with him." She winked as she said this, and I wondered if it was evil that I was setting up Leif for the most humiliating night of his life. An image of Gina's tear-swollen face flashed through my head, and I decided I was simply greasing the great karma machine in the sky.

Kennie promised to do the deeds as soon as she finished leading her "As Good as Gold" tour on the Otter Tail River. Apparently, the Minnesota Nice business wasn't doing as well as expected. People felt too guilty about hiring someone else to do their dirty work and decided to return to the tried-and-true practices of avoidance and denial.

To supplement her income, Kennie had launched a gold-panning business on the Otter Tail River. There was no gold in the water, hence the name of her business.

I promised to post her brochures at the library and go out on one more double date with her and Gary in exchange for her Minnesota Nice gig for me. Apparently, I'd gone over like gangbusters with Ody, and he wanted to take me fishing before he returned to Alaska. How much worse could my reputation in town get? At least I knew our time together had an expiration date.

I should have probably taken more time to heal before I went diving, but the need to satisfy my curiosity outweighed the drive to be pain-free. I borrowed Jed's diving equipment and got permission from the landowners to take off from the creek side of the lake. My bruises made swimming slow going, but eventually I found the camo netting about seventy-five feet straight out and twenty-one feet straight down, just like Nikolai predicted. If not for him, I would have passed right over it.

I wasn't able to open the box on my own, so I called the *Pioneer Press*. They ran a front-page story on the "Real Jewels of the North Country," and the featured photo was of Peyton draped in the treasure.

I felt momentarily bad that Nikolai wasn't getting any of the money for finding the box, and then I realized I'd promised him only that I would not keep more than half. By the end of the week, a "secret donor" had paid for paint for all the cabins at the Last Resort, inside and out. I also arranged for a deluxe Scrabble game, complete with a lazy Susan, to be sent to the Fortune Café. The children's section at the library got completely revamped as well—new chairs, new stuffed animals, new equipment for watching movies and listening to books on tape, and a cavalcade of happy, colorful new books.

Mysteriously, Peyton also received a colossal box of Sugar Lips Wax Chewing Gum, Strawberry Pop Rocks, Razzles Candy Gum, and chocolate cigarettes in the mail. I heard through the grapevine that Leylanda had loosened up a little on her daughter, and I hoped she'd let her keep the candy.

With the money that was left, I had just enough to hire a landscaper to do some touch-up work at my place. I called Swenson's Nursery, and Johnny promised he'd be over before the end of the week. I felt conspicuous enough requesting him specifically and after hours, so I refrained from offering extra for shirtlessness.

While I waited for him to show up on a beautiful Friday evening, I phoned my mom. When Peyton had been kidnapped, some more of my heart froze. What I hadn't known was how much it was going to thaw when she was found. My mom and I hadn't talked in more than a year, but there was something about worrying about kids and getting the ever-loving crap beaten out of you that made you want to hear your mom's voice.

"Mira?"

"Yeah. Sorry I haven't called in a while."

"How're you doing?" She sounded so grateful that it brought tears to my eyes.

"I've been pretty good. How about you?"

I heard her weigh her options, and she chose to keep it light, even though she couldn't hold the emotion out of her voice. I suppose she didn't want to scare me off again. "I'm real good. We're having a wedding shower for your cousin next weekend. We'd love to see you."

"Yeah, maybe. I'd like to see you, too." The funny thing was, I meant it. My mom and I had drifted apart after my dad died, no doubt about it. Or maybe I'd pushed her away. And maybe there was time to change that.

"You still have Tiger Pop?"

"Yeah, she's on my lap right now." I stroked my kitty's soft fur. "I'll give you a call about next weekend, 'kay?"

"That would be nice. I love you, Mira."

The tears were pouring down my face now. This had been a damn tough week, but my mom still loved me. I made my voice sound strong. "I love you, too, Mom." I clicked the phone off and dug my face into Tiger Pop's clean fur.

When Johnny showed up a half hour later, I was composed and wearing my sexiest natural-woman look—no makeup save for lip gloss, hair loose around my shoulders, a white tank top, and faded cutoffs. Figured there was no point in trying to hide the fading, greenish-yellow bruises on my face and arms. I was still stiff from the beating but feeling whole and strong. I hardly made a fool of myself the whole time Johnny was over.

He spent more time admiring my garden and giving me tips on improved water retention and maximization of sunlight than actually landscaping, but it was a wonderful evening. Once, I caught him staring at the rainbow of marks spattered across my face and neck. I had to glance away, the angry and protective look in his eyes too much for my emotional state.

I instead coaxed him to talk about himself. Turned out he wasn't kicked out of college, either for knifing someone or for stealing plants, though he did write his senior paper on the blade tree, native to Bolivia. He'd graduated fair and square and planned to go on to grad school to get his PhD. He'd seen himself as either a professor or an activist, but before he decided what college he wanted to do his doctoral work at, his dad had been diagnosed with terminal stomach cancer. Johnny returned to Battle Lake to help his mom take care of him and was making the best of his current life.

"Mira?"

I was walking him to his car. The sun was setting the lake on fire as it dropped, clouds of pink and orange rising like steam on the horizon.

"Yeah?"

"Can I ask you something personal?"

My stomach bubbled. I clenched my teeth to hold back the slew of dumb suddenly pushing to escape my mouth. "Sure."

"Are you dating Ody?"

I think I might have laughed, but it came out like a horse bark. "No. I was just doing Kennie a favor."

Johnny appeared relieved, then amused. He reached out as if to touch my face, shook his head once quickly, and stuffed his hands in his worn jean pockets. "I'm sorry someone did this to you, Mira."

My heart tumbled. "Thanks. But I'll heal. I always do."

He nodded, staring at the ground. "It was a good night, tonight. I had fun with you."

I smiled. "I had fun with you, too."

Johnny didn't give me a bill at the end of our wonderful evening, but immediately after he left, I wrote out a check and dropped it in the mailbox at the end of my mile of driveway, retrieving the day's mail at the same time. I wanted an excuse to walk down the road barefoot.

On my way back, I slowed to scratch my feet in the soft sand pool, an unexplained spot in every country driveway where the sand was so smooth it felt wet. I decided when I got back to the house that I'd eat a bowl of fresh peas, drink a Dr Pepper, and watch *Thelma and Louise*, one of three movies I owned.

And maybe, if I had the time, I'd draw Johnny's name over and over again in a notebook and sketch hearts around it.

It was such a good plan that I almost threw out the letter from the University of Minnesota before I even opened it. Instead, I studied the return address as I crunched down the gravel and smelled the dusty earth and listened to the crickets sing. The letter was from the U of M's English department. I'd withdrawn from the grad program right before I had moved to Battle Lake, and I didn't see how this could be good news.

Curiosity, my only consistent vice, won over, and when I reached my front deck, I sat down and ripped open the letter, my toes digging into the still-warm earth of my front flower bed.

The letter was from the one professor I had connected with at the university, Dr. Bundy. He was a lit prof who questioned everything and had a wonderfully dry sense of humor.

His note was short and sweet:

> Dear Mira:
> You are missed! I need a research assistant this fall, and you're my woman. Pay is meager, but your tuition would be free. Is it a deal? Respond at your convenience, as long as it's before August.
>   Sincerely yours,
>   Dr. Michael Bundy

I read it three times before I was convinced it wasn't a joke, and that's when I started to feel a little seasick. This would have been a no-brainer a month ago. An opportunity like this came once in a lifetime. Who wouldn't want to live in the Twin Cities and go to school for free and eat at restaurants that didn't serve hot beef and white bread as their specials?

But now, I wasn't so sure.

I stood up so abruptly that I scraped the back of my leg on the deck. I strode into the house purposefully, crumpled up Dr. Bundy's letter, and tossed it in the garbage. I opened the fridge, fixed myself supper, and stuck *Thelma and Louise* into the VCR.

I watched it until I was too tired to keep my eyes open, and then I popped off to bed, but not before I pulled Dr. Bundy's letter out of the garbage, smoothed it out, and set it on my kitchen table to look at again in the morning.

About the Author

Photo © 2023 Kelly Weaver Photography

Jess Lourey writes about secrets. She's the bestselling author of thrillers, comic caper mysteries, book club fiction, young adult fiction, and nonfiction. Winner of the Anthony, Thriller, and Minnesota Book Awards, Jess is also an Edgar, Agatha, and Lefty Award–nominated author; TEDx presenter; and recipient of The Loft's Excellence in Teaching fellowship. Check out her TEDx Talk for the true story behind her debut novel, *May Day*. She lives in Minneapolis with a rotating batch of foster kittens (and occasional foster puppies, but those goobers are a lot of work). For more information, visit www.jessicalourey.com.